FIVE HEARTS

Five Stories of Love and Passion

Sable Hunter
Cynthia Arsuaga
Dana Littlejohn
Daisy Dunn
Sandy Sullivan

Erotic Romance

Secret Cravings Publishing
www.secretcravingspublishing.com

A Secret Cravings Publishing Book
Erotic Romance

FIVE HEARTS – FIVE STORIES OF LOVE AND PASSION
Copyright © 2012 Cynthia Arsuaga, Dana Littlejohn, Sandy Sullivan, Daisy Dunn, Sable Hunter
Print ISBN: 978-1-61885-230-4

First E-book Publication: February 2012
First Print Publication: March 2012

Cover design by Dawne Dominique
Edited by Stephanie Balestreri
Proofread by Ariana Gaynor
All cover art and logo copyright © 2012 by Secret Cravings Publishing

ALL RIGHTS RESERVED: This literary work may not be reproduced or transmitted in any form or by any means, including electronic or photographic reproduction, in whole or in part, without express written permission.

All characters and events in this book are fictitious. Any resemblance to actual persons living or dead is strictly coincidental.
PUBLISHER
Secret Cravings Publishing
www.secretcravingspublishing.com

Five Hearts – Five Stories of Love and Passion

The Cravings e-book Club
The Cravings Paranormal e-book Club

Have you heard about the newest idea in ebooks, the ebook club? Secret Cravings Publishing has started two ebook clubs and we invite you to become a member of either The Cravings e-book Club or the Cravings Paranormal e-book Club. Join now and get two books absolutely free!

As a member, you will receive *Taming The Cougar** by Sandy Sullivan and *Hunting Jaguar*** by D. McEntire FREE, just for joining!

You'll also receive **4 BRAND-NEW EBOOKS**, specially selected by our Editorial Director, every month for a total price of only $9.99 for all 4. This comes out to barely $2.50 per book, much less than the retail price and you'll be able to enjoy your books *even before* they hit Amazon or Barnes & Noble. We send your books *before* they are uploaded to the popular sales sites. One of several privileges of club membership.

**Taming the Cougar*, a western, erotic romance:*
Marla isn't looking for love or anything else from a man. Can Marla put aside her distrust of men for a younger man? Can Chris convince her he's not like other guys?

**Hunting Jaguar, paranormal erotic romance:*

Rachel Hayes' Father set out to prove the existence of the Miloni temple and the Jaguar people. Tumi is a descendant of the Miloni race and is sworn to protect their secret with his life. Will he be forced to uphold his vow at the cost of his heart and Rachel's life?

As a member of the Cravings Club, you'll receive 4 books in a variety of genres every month. We will try to match your books to your preferences, however, if you're a major paranormal fan, I suggest you join the Cravings Paranormal Club. Everything is the same, 4 books every month for $9.99 except that 3 of your 4 books will be paranormal. The remaining book will be of a different genre.

As a club member, you will also receive:
- our monthly newsletter
- sneak previews of new books
- exclusive interviews with your favorite authors
- special offers not available to the general public

To join and tell us your favorite genres and heat levels plus which format works best for you, go to the Secret Cravings Publishing website (www.secretcravingspublishing.com) At the bottom of the page you'll see a button for the club. You can sign up there and share your preferences for genre, format and heat level with us. You will be charged, automatically, through PayPal, only $9.99 every month. Your books will be shipped within 1 day after PayPal payment has cleared. You may cancel at any time by clicking on the "unsubscribe" button located on the Cravings Club tab at the bottom of our website and keep the FREE BOOKS as our gift.

We hope our Secret Cravings books will delight you each and every month.

Best wishes,
Beth Walker

A Hot And Spicy Valentine
by
Sable Hunter

"If there's anything in the world wrong with that man I can't see it." Dorothy elbowed Riley almost knocking her off the bar stool.

"What's supposed to be wrong with him?" Riley wasn't up on island gossip, she had always had too many problems of her own to worry about.

"They say he can't talk."

After dropping that bombshell, Dorothy leaned over and started flirting with Chad, another employee of the hot sauce factory where everyone at their table worked. This was trivia night at Get Down Brown's and Riley had been invited because she knew more useless information than anyone else at Beaucoup. No one would ask her to dance; they never had and tonight wouldn't be any different.

Riley mulled over Dorothy's statement. Seth Walker, the man in question, was easily the handsomest man she had ever seen. He was big and powerful looking, his back broad enough to bear the weight of the world. Riley tried to imagine what kind of a voice a man like that might have. If she closed her eyes, she could almost hear him speaking to her. His tone would be husky and warm and send shivers down her spine. Yes, it would be a shame for a voice like that to be quieted. "Not at all?" She put her hand on Dorothy's arm to get her attention.

It took a second for her friend to realize what she was being asked. "He stutters, Riley. He stammers like your brother Bucky did." Dorothy's expression brightened. "Hey, maybe you could help him like you did Bucky. You ought to go offer your services. That would be one way you could put all of those classes you've been taking to good use." Her friend was sincere, but Riley had been teased enough about her ambition. So, she had a lot of time on her hands. Fat girls didn't get asked out on dates, they had to find other ways to make the hours pass.

Riley studied, puttered around her house, and fantasized about a man who would walk into her life and sweep her off her feet. So far, the studying and puttering had paid off, but the fantasies were all in her head. Taking a drink from her strawberry daiquiri, Riley realized it tasted bitter—probably because guilt accompanied every sip. She should have stuck to Diet Dr Pepper. Lord knows she didn't need the extra calories. Considering Seth, she came to the obvious conclusion. "He's the boss's son. I'm sure he's had all the medical attention money can buy."

Dorothy just shrugged as if there was something she wasn't telling.

The disc jockey, Scott, came to the microphone. Two girls hung onto him, both wearing more perfume than clothing. "We have one last question ladies and gentlemen. This is for a round of drinks." He paused to raise suspense. "Beaucoup, as always, has won the most. That's because of their secret weapon." Scott looked right at her. For some reason, he had taken a dislike to Riley. They had grown up together, and for the life of her, she couldn't determine why he hated her so. It wasn't unusual to be teased, especially when you looked like Riley, but his animosity had gone beyond that.

His attitude toward her almost made her stay home. But tonight was about more than trivia—tonight was the big test. She was going to ask every unattached man in the place to dance—except Scott—and if no one took her up on it, she was going to take Mrs. Boone's advice and relocate. She could still hear her kind voice. "Riley," she had said, "you've lost weight and you're beautiful. But these small town hicks will never see you any differently. If you moved to a bigger town, you'd be treated like the goddess you are." *Goddess, right.* Riley didn't expect royal treatment, all she wanted was a bit of kindness and maybe a date every once in a while.

Riley waited on the question from Scott, and when it came, she knew it was a trap. Scott looked smug and asked in a sing-song voice. "This is the season of hearts and flowers. So, let's have a Valentine question. Who can tell me—for a round of drinks—what is a vinegar valentine?"

There was silence in the bar. Everyone from Beaucoup turned to her and she knew she couldn't let them down—no matter how Scott chose to embarrass her. Chad and Ronny and Michael were all staring at her, waiting. Slowly she raised her hand.

"Of course, Ms. Jacobs. I knew you would have the answer. I bet you've received several vinegar valentines yourself. Come on up and join me, so everyone can hear your knowledgeable answer."

Riley stood up and slowly walked to the podium like she was making her way to the gallows. Seth Walker turned and looked at her. She gave him a small smile, wondering if he knew who she was. If he didn't already he would soon. *Great!* This was the story of her life. She always got to bear the brunt of someone else's joke.

Riley took the microphone from Scott, who waited with a shit-eating grin on his face. So, she gave him the right answer. "A vinegar valentine is one that contains an insult instead of a message of affection." Then she waited for the other shoe to drop. She didn't have long to wait.

Talking in the condescending tone he reserved only for her, the disc jockey bellowed his announcement. "Beaucoup wins a round of drinks, everybody. And as for you, Miss Jacobs—roses are red, violets are blue, no one is fatter or uglier than you. I bet that's the only kind of valentine you've ever received. Am I correct?" There it was. Scott delivered the blow so smoothly; it was obvious he had put a lot of thought into hurting her.

Riley stood there for a moment and let the words slide through her mind. Paralyzed, she knew she needed to head back to her chair, but she couldn't make her feet move. She looked at Scott, wide-eyed, as if waiting for another punch. Even the band was between songs. No one had missed her humiliation. She heard whispers, snickers, and a few pained gasps. Mortified, Riley was about to thank him and take her leave—though her mind was still frozen—when he was hoisted off the ground and hung dangling with the tips of his boots just dragging the dusty floor.

"Need glasses, idiot?" The words were stilted and forced, but they sounded like music to Riley's heart. Seth Walker had come to her rescue, picking up the DJ like he was a straw scarecrow. Scott kicked his legs weakly, but Seth held him aloft with ease.

Riley looked up and up at her savior, he must be at least six foot five—a formidable figure of a man. "Thank you, so much. I'm Riley

Jacobs. I think I work for you. I'm the company nurse." She held her hand out to him, in greeting.

He dropped Scott like a sack of potatoes, and the DJ staggered trying to find his footing. Seth turned, standing between Riley and the rude man like a big windbreak that could keep the coldest of winter chills at bay. Slowly, he picked up her outstretched hand, stroked a thumb across her palm and brought the back of her hand to his lips.

Riley felt the gentle caress of his kiss and she wanted to melt into a puddle at his feet.

Seth looked like he wanted to say something. He opened his mouth, but nothing came out.

She was about to excuse herself, but he took his other hand and began to sign.

"Can you read sign language?" At her excited nod, he continued. "Hello, Riley. It's a pleasure to meet you. My name is Seth Walker. Would you do me the honor of dancing with me?"

"Me?" Riley looked up at Seth, then glanced behind her. "You want to dance with me? Are you sure?"

She watched him try and form a response. His beautiful face clouded with frustration, then looked sadly resigned. "Please?" He formed the word with his fingers.

There was no way she would tell him no. Even if he was doing it because he felt sorry for her, which was most likely the case, she couldn't run the risk of hurting his feelings. What if he were sincere? He would think she had turned him down because he had trouble speaking. "I'm not very good, but I would love to try." A beautiful smile lit up his face and Riley was struck by how gorgeous he was. He had navy blue eyes, dark lashes, black hair and a smile that was as contagious as chicken pox. This man could have any woman he wanted, but for a few minutes he was going to belong to Riley Jacobs. This might turn out to be a Happy Valentine's after all.

* * * *

Seth offered her his arm. What in the hell was he doing? How could he make this work? There was a reason he didn't come to places like this. And there was a damn good reason he didn't date beautiful girls like Riley. He seldom kept company with women, mainly because he couldn't string enough words together to build a decent size sentence. Oh, there were always women willing to overlook his handicap because he was wealthy, but sooner or later they let their disgust shine through, not a lot of women wanted to bed a man who sounded like Mel Tillis or Porky Pig. But, paying for sex wasn't his style, either. Unfortunately, Seth was cursed with a giant appetite for sex and not a lot of opportunities to satisfy it. Right now, his cock was awake, hard, throbbing and rarin' to go. Little Riley was the sweetest morsel he had been this close to in many a day and if he blew this his dick might file suit on him for breach of promise.

Damn! The top of her head only came to his shoulder. She was a pint-sized Venus with more curves than a roller coaster, which was exactly what he felt like he was on. Taking over Beaucoup was a big step for him and moving back to Egret Island was a decision he had questioned more than once in the past month. Meeting a little doll like Riley could make the upheaval in his life a whole lot easier to endure.

"Thanks for rescuing me." She stood on tiptoes and whispered in his ear as he pulled her into his embrace. The dance floor was crowded and the music was faster than he would have liked, but he intended to take advantage of the circumstances and cuddle this sweetie while he had the chance. If only he could sign and dance at the same time, but that was impossible. By the time he got through stammering in her ear, she would bid him the time of day as fast as the other women he had dared to try and date.

Hell! "Wel…Wel…Welcome." *Finally*. By the time he choked out the word, he was growling at her like a bear. Reflex made him grab her closer and just for a second she stiffened, and then to Seth's surprise, Riley sank all of those soft curves into his body like she was coming home. And when she sighed and laid her head on his chest, he knew that she could hear his heart pounding like an overeager school boy.

"This is so nice. I've never danced with a man before—only my broom." He felt her giggle and all of that sweet tit flesh pushed against him. Were those her nipples he could feel? *Hell yeah!* Hard little buttons were pressing greedily against his chest. He knew there was no way she was missing his cock—it was fully engaged in the situation and wanting to negotiate terms and conditions.

Seth gritted his teeth and counted to ten—forcing the words out between clenched teeth. "Good…" he grunted. "Like. Dance. You." He frowned. Any minute now, she would excuse herself and head for the bathroom. He knew the drill.

Where was the safety of his Wall Street office where he could communicate via memo or with his computer dictation program? This was the age of texting and emails—the best time a man like him could hope to live in. He had often wished humans communicated strictly by the written word. Thanks to Harvard, he was more than proficient at expressing himself in prose. He had two college degrees to prove it.

"I like to dance with you too."

Several people were watching them closely, and he didn't sneer at them, but he did glance at them with dismissive authority. He knew how to be the big boss and it wasn't too early to make his presence known in this small, reclusive island community that had been his family's home for generations. One of his first orders of business was to make sure whatever game these people had been playing with this small doll was going to be over and through with. He had watched her all evening and when everybody was being asked to dance, she had been passed over time and time again. He hadn't understood it. She sat there with that expectant little look of hope each time a man came to their table and when another woman—one less attractive—was led away, she had only looked resigned, not surprised. What was wrong with these people?

Instead of answering her, he played a bold card and kissed her on the temple. She smelled like spiced peaches, one of his favorite things in the whole world. On this island, any smell other than the spicy hot peppers that were grown here was unusual. The fragrant, fiery smell permeated everything, but it had made his family wealthy and had spawned a legacy that had existed since before the Civil War. Beaucoup sauce was made on Egret Island and shipped literally all over the world.

"I love this," she spoke softly. "You've single-handedly saved my reputation from being an undateable, fat frump. And you didn't even have to take me out—you did it with one dance." There was no bitterness; it was like Riley was just stating a fact.

This time he shook his head before he tried to enunciate the simple word "N…N…No!" His whole body tensed up at the effort and he felt his erection subsiding. *Great*. And when she pulled back in his arms, he was expecting her to turn tail and run. But, she didn't.

Instead, the look on her face was one of confusion. "What was the 'no' for? No, this isn't a date? Don't worry. I realize that." When he shook his head saying she was wrong, she gave him the sweetest smile. "If it's about your speech, don't be embarrassed. I have a brother that speaks as you do, and I know something that might help." Seth narrowed his eyes, listening. She continued. "Would you mind a suggestion?"

That's right, he remembered, she was a nurse. But what could a small town medical worker know that the great doctors on the East Coast did not? On the other hand, what did he have to lose? Plus, he got to spend a little extra time with a beautiful woman—it seemed like a win/win to him. Taking one hand off her shoulder, he signed between them. "I'll take all the help I can get. This affliction puts a damper on my life, especially my love life." Lord, she was pretty. "What color are your eyes?"

"A washed out purple color, violet, I think." Leaning close, she whispered conspiratorially, "It worked with my brother, so let's try it with you."

Seth bent down so he wouldn't miss a word she had to say.

"If you'll whisper, I think you will be able to speak a little easier. I know it doesn't work with everyone, but it might help you with your women."

Seth couldn't help but chuckle, she looked so sincere. And when was the last time he had ever heard of a woman being willing to help a man attract other women? Hell, why not. He'd give it a try. *Shit*! He was nervous. What would he say? Putting his head right at her ear, he mouthed the words—not even attempting to engage his vocal cords beyond the barest minimum. "You sure are pretty," he offered. The spoken word had always been his enemy. So only on occasion had he tried to whisper, mostly when he was groaning and pleasuring himself. And then he hadn't really paid any attention to what he sounded like. Had she heard him?

She had. But she didn't look happy. "You don't have to say that. I know I'm not pretty."

"Not pretty—beautiful," he whispered again.

This time it hit her. She bounced in his arms. "You did it!" When she was happy, there were two of the most intriguing dimples next to her mouth. "I'm so happy!"

He was happy too. And right now he wanted to show her exactly how happy he was. Not caring how he sounded—he almost shouted. "Let's go!" Oddly enough, the louder he talked, the easier the words came out. That quirk didn't do a lot for his asshole reputation but so be it. He didn't wait to see if she would follow, he took her by the hand and pulled.

"Okay, okay. I'm coming," she said breathlessly as she managed to keep up.

Yea, she was going to come—and come soon, if he had anything to do with it. God, he hoped she felt the same way he did. He hadn't been this attracted to a woman in a long time. Seth felt her bump into a couple of people and slowed down to gather her close. He was letting his excitement cloud his good judgment. He made his way out of the crowded bar and into the South Louisiana night. Even though it was the middle of February, you couldn't exactly call the weather cold—it was nippy, but pleasant.

"Where are we going?" she asked.

It was dark, so signing wouldn't work. So Seth tried his new trick. He stopped, pulled her sweet, lush body up to his and whispered in her ear. Riley wasn't his usual type, but being with her felt right. He wasn't ready to get serious with anybody, but he sure would like some playtime—if she was interested that is. "Island. I want to spend time with you. Okay?"

* * * *

Okay? Was he kidding? "Spending time with you sounds good to me." Frankly, Riley couldn't believe how the evening was turning out. She had gone to trivia night with the others, just so they'd win a few rounds of drinks. It had been her original plan to ask a few men to dance, and if they had all turned her down, she would have taken that as a sign it was time to venture out of Egret Island and see what the rest of the world had to offer a former fat girl with no self-confidence to speak of. Instead, she was running off into the night with the most handsome man she had ever laid eyes on, and he seemed happy to be with her. Perhaps, he even desired her. *God!* That was a wild thought! Tomorrow was Valentine's Day, usually the saddest and most lonely day of the year for her. But not this year—maybe.

"Car?" he asked bluntly and loudly. Riley knew from dealing with Bucky most people who stuttered could talk more plainly the louder they spoke. Winston Churchill was a prime example of that. Most of the world never knew he had struggled with a speech problem. Now, what had he said? Car? She hesitated a moment until she realized he was enquiring whether she had come in her own vehicle.

"No, I rode with Dorothy." Seth led her to a big, black truck. She smiled; it looked like him—commanding, mysterious and powerful. Opening the passenger door, he picked her up and she moaned a bit, not because it hurt, but because she couldn't ever remember being picked up, at least not since she was a toddler. "I'm too heavy."

At her declaration, he stepped close, his big form blocking the light of the moon. Cupping her face, he whispered, "Stop. You are delectable." Chills surged through her as she felt his breath and then his lips on her neck, causing every nerve ending in her body to tingle, especially the ones between her legs. Riley felt her clit swell and her pussy began to pulse with anticipation. Would he want to make love to her? Would she let him? Saying she was attracted to him was a huge understatement. And a chance like this had never come before, and Lord knows how long it would be before it happened again. So, yeah, she hoped to high heaven he wanted her enough to introduce her to the magic of sex. Riley wanted to ask for it—to beg—but she couldn't. She did have some pride. But if he offered she would be on him like white on rice.

Riley sat perfectly still and let Seth do exactly as he pleased. She was afraid to breathe; afraid he would stop kissing her neck. She closed her eyes and tilted her head up, offering him full access. Her nipples were so hard and achy, she wished she were brave enough to play with them herself or ask him to do it for her. He kissed a hot path up her neck, taking little nibbles and sucks as he went along. Once, she even felt the scrape of his teeth as he made his way to her mouth. "Please…" she found herself whispering. A second before he reached her mouth, she relented and turned—just enough—to meet his kiss.

"Mmmmmm," he groaned, capturing her lips. Her hands crept around his neck. She didn't have to think or worry, all she had to do was feel. Seth took control. He sucked at her bottom lip and ran his tongue around the edge in sweet little licks. She couldn't resist, she let her tongue find his. She wanted to play too.

"Yeah," he growled as he sealed their lips, thrusting his tongue deep, eating at her mouth with a hunger Riley completely understood. When his hand slipped between them and cupped a breast, she thought she was going to orgasm right then and there. Pushing her tit into his hand, Riley let him know—wordlessly—that she welcomed his touch.

"You like that?" he murmured, seemingly with ease. She took that as a compliment, he was into her and enjoying it, so his stress level was lower and he stuttered less.

Riley stopped trying to analyze his speech patterns, and just enjoyed the experience. "God, yes. More, please." And when Seth pinched her nipple, she jerked and felt a rush of cream flow from her hot core.

A loud whistle broke through the haze of their passion and Riley heard Seth's frustrated "Fuck!" She smiled a secret smile. He had no trouble with that word, and she would bet her life that he had no trouble with the act itself. In fact, she had no doubt Seth was a master at pleasuring a woman.

His obvious frustration at having their petting session cut short gave Riley a form of courage she had not known she possessed. "Let's go to my place. We'll be more comfortable there. If you'd like to that is," she offered tentatively.

His only answer was a hard kiss and him turning her, tenderly, arranging her in the seat and fastening the seat belt. Riley had never felt like this, so taken care of. No man had ever taken time with her, or touched her or made her feel desired. Seth stole one more kiss before he shut the truck door and climbed into the driver's seat.

It was too dark to see him sign and the engine was too loud to hear him whisper, so Riley decided to do the talking just to fill any awkward, empty silence. If they were going to spend some time together, she wanted him to feel as comfortable as possible. "I'm sure there have been a lot of changes here since you've been gone." She wasn't sure how often he had visited—or even if he had. Not waiting for him to answer, she went on. "My office is in the factory and sometimes I help with the tours. This year, we're—you're, I guess—giving big baskets of food for Valentine's Day. Most companies give at Thanksgiving and Christmas, but Beaucoup decided to add this to their list of benevolent acts. And I'm in charge of that, I add homemade cookies and crafts to the packages. I love helping out where I can, it makes me feel like I have a purpose."

She could tell he was glancing over at her, but she didn't allow any lulls in the conversation that would make him feel like he had to respond. "People love to come and visit your home. I know you are aware that almost every worker at Beaucoup was born on Egret Island. Last week an erotic romance writer came to tour the whole island. Her boyfriend, I guess, came with her and they brought their dog. Dorothy was really nice to her and gathered up a lot of history of the island and your great grandfather to give her. When Dorothy asked her what she wrote, she said she's writing a romance set on Egret Island and that it will be as hot and spicy as our peppers. Isn't that funny?" She giggled. "An erotic romance, yes, that I want to read." Hesitating, she fanned herself. Just thinking about a sexy book reminded her how much she would love to have sex with Seth.

To take her mind off of her creaming girly parts, she talked more about the writer. "They stayed and ate with us and Dorothy even gave the little dog—his name was Mojo—a wiener." Riley laughed. "Can you imagine—a wiener for a wiener dog?" It was too dark to see his face, so she didn't know if was enjoying her banter or not. "I love to go down in the jungle gardens. I walk down there almost every day. I know that you know we're not supposed to feed the alligators, but I swear one of them is almost tame. I call him Elvis, because I love Elvis and that's what Don

Johnson named his alligator on his TV show," she paused. "I can't remember the name of the show."

Riley almost jumped when Seth placed a big hand on her knee and began massaging her leg, causing ripples of arousal to weave their way up to her vagina. "Sw-Sw-Sweet," he said, slowly. "Know what…doing." She understood that he appreciated her efforts to make their journey easier on them both.

New Iberia was only seven miles from Egret Island, so they really didn't have that far to go. When they crossed the bridge over the Petit Chene Bayou, Riley got really, really excited. Would he make love to her? "I live at the end of White Heron Lane." She didn't have to tell him where that was; after all, he grew up here. Seth was several years older than Riley, so she had to admit she had no real memories of him at all. He had left the island and went to boarding school at an early age, while she had stayed here and been the girl everybody picked on. There was a child like that in every school, and she had been Egret Island's unfortunate one.

Actually, she was relieved Seth hadn't gone to school with her—at least he had no memory of her when she was really fat, she hoped. Growing up, her mom had equated food with happiness, love and celebration. Riley had been well loved and had done a lot of celebrating, but she had never been truly happy. It was only when she had moved out of her parent's house that the weight had melted off, but by then her image as the chubby girl was so engrained in everyone's mind that no one saw her as anything else. All of the guys were afraid to date her, afraid they would be ridiculed for dating Round Riley. At times she caught some of them looking at her with heat in their eyes, but they never approached her. And that was why Mrs. Boone had suggested she leave the island. Now, she was glad she had waited, at least for a little while.

As the truck eased to a stop in her driveway, Riley was shaking like a leaf. She started to open her door, but a hand to a shoulder and a whispered, "Wait," caused her to stop. What for? He gestured to the door and Riley understood he wanted to help her exit the vehicle. She couldn't help but smile. This was going to be so good. Whatever the night had to offer, she was going to be grateful because it was so much more than she had ever hoped for.

Seth helped her out, took her hand, and walked with her to the small Louisiana cottage she called home. He stood aside while she let them in, but all the while he was scratching her back—up and down—long slow strokes that had every part of her reacting. Both nipples were swelling and puffing out, her clit was getting hard and beginning to throb. Riley was so turned on, she was afraid she was going to combust.

Opening the door, she walked in ahead of him, welcoming him into her home. Wow, she thought—he was the first man, other than her dad, who had ever been here. This was virgin territory. At that Riley almost choked. Virgin territory, there was a lot of that around—namely her. She turned on the lights and revealed to Seth a glimpse into her personality.

There were several telling factors if he picked up on them. First, she loved the color blue—all shades. Blues mixed with fern greens and earth tones, the colors of the island were everywhere. And second, Riley loved animals and she collected prints and statues, not cheap knockoffs but pieces local artists from South Louisiana had created. They weren't costly, but they were precious. There were full-sized wooden carvings of birds, cats and even a small alligator sitting on her table and hearth. And the walls were covered with prints depicting area swamp scenes and plantations. Lastly—it was comfortable—there was no put-on in her house.

Riley had decorated her home, not for friends or company, she had decorated it for herself and hoped Seth would feel at home with her. *Whoa*! She pulled herself back, mentally. This was—couldn't be—anything but a one-night stand. After all, she was Riley Jacobs, fat little nobody. And Seth was South Louisiana royalty—rich, handsome as sin and so far out of her league they weren't even playing the same game. Irregardless. "Welcome."

"Your home looks like you," he signed with a smile. He meant it as a compliment, she could tell, so she took it that way.

"Do you want something to drink?" she asked. Wasn't that what people said in situations like this?

"No." Seth didn't say the word out loud, he mouthed it as he stalked her, literally stalked her, across the room.

She had never seen that kind of look on a man's face before, not directed at her anyway. She backed up a step, he was damned intimidating. And then she stopped. Was she crazy? He was magnificent.

No one could look at him and tell he had money, but they sure could tell he was all male. A starched white Western shirt caressed every single, delineated muscle. The shirt wasn't skin-tight, but it did showcase the goods, just right. And those jeans—Riley had never felt the need to genuflect to a pair of blue jeans before, but these pants were covering holy ground. And she had a sudden urge to visit the Promised Land. *Holy Shit!* All of her Catholic Bible stories were coming out in smutty blue prose. Next she would be waiting on the 'rapture' to come.

"Would you like to get more comfortable?" *Shoot!* That wasn't what she was supposed to say. He smiled, and her heart melted. What was she supposed to say? "Should I put on something more comfortable?" Yep, this was a bad idea. Riley watched his face change until he looked more amused than aroused. Damn, time to tell the truth. "You do realize I'm not any good at this don't you?"

* * * *

She had no idea how adorable she was. How he wished he could say everything he was thinking. Riley looked like the sweetest cotton candy. She wore light pink jeans, a pink lace camisole, pink tennis shoes and a pink sparkly ribbon was braided in her hip length dark hair. Seth had no idea he was so fond of pink. He wondered if her nipples and pussy were that same luscious shade. Walking right up to her, he was surprised she stood her ground. Much preferring the whispering to the signing, he just did what it took to make himself happy, he picked her up and walked off with her. "Where's the bed?" he whispered in her ear.

"Up the stairs and to the right."

So, he took off. About a half second later, she stiffened up in his arms like a young goat he had raised when he was a boy. That goat had hated to be picked up and would become like a wooden statue in protest.

"Put me down, Seth. I'm too heavy to tote up the stairs."

"Shhhh," he soothed her as he found her bedroom. This time he didn't look at décor, he had better things to look at. Laying her on her bed, he turned on the bedside lamp so there would be light enough. He wanted there to be no mistaking what he said. And he wanted to see her curvy little body more than he wanted to see the sun rise.

"Do you want this?" he asked with a few deft movements of his hand. Seth held his breath, he needed this, he needed her. She gave him a quiet acceptance few people ever had, and he loved the way that felt.

"Yes." Riley didn't mince her words. But he did see she was thinking, considering, and what she said next floored him. "Are you sure you want me? You're not teasing me, are you? This isn't a joke like what Scott would pull?" Her big eyes filled with tears and almost brought him to his knees. "If you undressed me and then laughed at how I looked, it would kill me."

Seth did the only thing that seemed right. He went to his knees at her feet, picked up both of her hands in his and kissed them. Letting them go, he began to sign. "Baby, I can tell people have been cruel to you. I am so sorry." He feathered a touch down her face with one finger, caressing her cheek. "I wish you could see what I see, a gorgeous face with big eyes and the sexiest lips I've ever kissed. And your body, Riley, you look like what a woman is supposed to look like, round in all the right places, I can't wait to see all of you." When the tip of a pink tongue darted out to moisten her upper lip, he couldn't resist. She tasted so good, he fit his mouth to hers and just sucked at her sweetness. When he pulled back, she followed him, obviously wanting more. He was happy to oblige, his lips slid over hers in a long, slow tease. And when she whimpered, he chuckled.

"Don't laugh." She stiffened.

"Awww," he whispered right against her ear. "I'm not laughing at you, baby. I'm just happy. You make me happy." And she did, she was totally open, there wasn't a trace of judgment in the way she treated him. "I can't keep my hands off you. Can I have your breasts now?" Seth sat back and waited to see what she would do.

Riley didn't disappoint, she held his gaze and picked up the bottom of her lace camisole pulling it over her head.

Swear to God, Seth held his breath. "Damn," he murmured.

"My bra isn't fancy. I wish I had sexier underwear."

Her hands fell to her side and she kept her eyes downcast. That was just as well, she didn't need to see him drool. *Holy fuck*! His hands actually shook as he reached around her to unhook her bra. Trying to convey how privileged he felt, he kissed her shoulder, inhaling the sweet peaches and cream fragrance of her skin. Pulling the cups down, his mouth began to water. He had to say it—it had to be said—pushing out the word, he declared. "Per–perfect." Round, high, full. Riley had luscious, creamy tits with big puffy pink nipples that visibly hardened as he traced them with a finger. A whimper of pure need slipped through her lips and Seth had to fight for control.

Vowing to take it slow, he kissed the pulse that fluttered at her throat. Sliding his lips across skin softer than any silk, he finally allowed himself to pay homage to the generous mounds. It was all he could do not to immediately latch onto a nipple, but he wanted her to realize how precious she was. Instead he took it slow, twirling his tongue around a puffy aureole, moaning as he rubbed his bristled jaw against the velvet tit.

She gasped and sighed, pushing her breast toward his lips. "Kiss me, Seth. I need you, so." She didn't need to beg, there was nothing he wanted more in the world. Opening his mouth wide over one nipple, he began to suckle hard. Riley cried out his name as he pulled with his lips and kneaded and milked with his hands. "God," she screamed. Her excitement and joy almost pushed him over the edge. Seth had never been hungrier for a woman. He feasted on one pink berry and then the other, going back and forth, until he finally pushed them together and teased them both at the same time.

* * * *

Riley needed to come, bad. Seth was subjecting her to the sweetest torture she could imagine. "Please." What was she begging for? Her hips wanted to lift, as if they wanted to buck. She wanted to be naked and she wanted Seth on top of her, in her. "Can we…do more?"

"Hmmmm," Seth growled as he began unsnapping her jeans. He pushed her back on the bed and stood watching as she began to slip them off, shedding her panties at the same time. Tremulously, Riley waited to see how he would react to the rest of her body. Her hips were wider than was fashionable and her bottom was round and full. He didn't say anything, he didn't have to, his eyes said it all. They were hooded, heated and she felt like she was drowning in their blue depths. All she could think was, *what a way to go*.

When he pulled off his shirt, she lost all ability to think. *Damn*! His muscles had muscles. She held her hands out, needing to touch. He shed his pants and lowered his body so she could satisfy her hunger and her curiosity. Seth groaned when she ran her palms over his chest, and as she began to trace the ripples and ridges with her tongue, he grabbed her hands and held them over her head.

"Lu–Lu–losing control," he ground out the words. He licked a trail from the tip of her nose, down the valley of her cleavage, over the roundness of her tummy, to the top of her mound.

Riley was so lost in passion that she didn't even think, she did something she could have never imagined being bold enough to do, she opened her legs wide, and offered Seth her pussy. Would he think her too brazen? Was she asking for something he didn't want to give?

Riley held her breath as Seth stared at her sex. She didn't have to wait long for an answer, because he licked his lips and fell to his knees, pulling her to the edge of the bed. With tiny kisses, he drew out her agony, kissing the inside of her trembling thigh. Never had she dreamed a man would go down on her, on Riley Jacobs! She didn't know whether to bolt and run or lay back and enjoy it. But when Seth gave her slit one quick lick that made her arch, she made up her mind, laying back and enjoying was the only sane thing to do.

Big hands spread her wide and when he nuzzled his face in her pussy and began kissing and sucking, she moaned and he shuddered. Shuddered? For a moment she doubted he was as into it as she was. Was she disgusting? Did she taste bad? But when she rose up and looked at his face, that notion flew out the window. Seth was obviously aroused. Riley had never known how mind-blowing it would be to see a man like Seth with his face in her pussy, enjoying it and pushing her toward a climax so fast it was like riding a runaway mine train.

* * * *

Seth was mad with desire. He wanted to fuck! God, his cock was so full of cum he was humping the side of the bed. The only thing that held him back was Riley. She was special and he would deny himself in favor of tasting her climax on his tongue first, even if it killed him. He made himself at home in her molten core, kissing softly between her plump lips. Riley's pussy quivered against his face, she liked what he was doing and that pleased him. Spearing his tongue deep in her channel, Seth fucked her, finding satisfaction when she keened loudly, her whole body jerking with delight. He anchored her with one hand pressing on her stomach, and for a few moments, he was lost in the wonder of this woman's pleasure.

There was nothing fake about Riley, she responded like a firebrand to his touch and he loved it. Flicking his tongue against her hot button, he pushed two fingers deep into her sex and sought out the spongy spot that would make her scream. It didn't take long, her snug little cunt clamped down tight and a few laves and licks with his tongue on her clit was all it took to make her explode, "Seth, My God, Seth!"

Watching her come, and feeling her pussy pulse against him was almost too much. He had to have relief and he had to have it now. Taking his cock, he rubbed it up and down her slit, bathing in her cream. He was just about to ram home, when she came to her knees and closed her palm around him.

"Let me, please. I want to do this for you. I love the way you look, you're so big." He started to protest, but when she enclosed the tip of his dick in her hot little mouth, he was lost. She sucked him. God, she was voracious. It was as if she were pouring a lifetime of want and need into the act of loving him. She took him deep, licking and laving, and he was undone. Grasping the back of her head, he encouraged her with grunts and growls. No words were necessary, he showed his appreciation by pulling at her nipples and massaging her tits.

Seth couldn't remember enjoying a woman more. Her little fingers found his sac and she rubbed and caressed and as he exploded, she wouldn't be pushed away. Instead she swallowed every drop and the look of absolute bliss on her face was almost as good as the rush of ecstasy that sent his seed shooting from his loins. And when she rubbed her face against his cock, kissing the shaft, an odd feeling of warmth flooded through him.

"Riley, baby," he whispered. He could feel himself hardening again and making love to her now seemed like the most important thing in his world. So, when his cell phone went off and the ring was the emergency signal from the factory, Seth was bitterly disappointed.

He grabbed the phone and after a few terse words, he learned one of the main pumps had blown a gasket and his presence was required. The foreman was on vacation and he knew how he handled this situation would set the tone for his tenure as boss.

"You have to go?" Riley asked with her heart in her eyes.

"Y-Y-Yea." He began to dress, pausing to answer her in sign. "There's a malfunction with some of the equipment. I'm sorry." Even in his satisfied state, he hungered for her. She had the most beautiful body, and she was sweet and kind. Seth wanted more. "How about if I give you a call tomorrow and we can make plans? It'll be Valentine's Day and we can do something special."

He watched her sit back on her heels and try to look okay with this abrupt change in plans. "Sure, I understand."

Seth couldn't help it, he went to her, rubbing his hands down her arms, across her breasts and lastly cupping her face as he kissed her deeply and passionately. "This isn't over, Riley. I will call, I promise."

* * * *

Last night had been fun. Riley tried to count her blessings. Seth had been sweet and kind and had given her the very best orgasm of her life. She was still a virgin, but he had said he would call. After he had left, she had lain in her lonely bed and rubbed herself on the sheets, inhaling his scent and dreaming he was there with her. As the hours had past, the whole thing seemed like a dream. If it hadn't been for the marks he had left on her body, the nips and sucks on her neck and on her thighs, Riley could have convinced herself it had all been a fantasy.

Would he call? She prayed that he would, but she prepared herself for the let-down. It was just her nature. Today was Saturday, Valentine's Day and she was off from work. With no special plans, she had all the time in the world to remember the bliss Seth had given her with his mouth and hands and how she had longed to learn what a man's full possession would feel like. How was it going to be to work with him every day? Would it be awkward?

As the hours passed, Riley baked cookies and finished the baskets, then set out to deliver them. She didn't own a cell phone, so leaving the house was hard. What if he called? What if he didn't? Tired of worrying and wondering, she loaded her car and set out to deliver the food offerings to the elderly and the shut-ins. Being the face of Beaucoup's benevolence program was always a joy to her, and soon that feeling returned. Spreading love and good will was always good for the soul.

The only sour spot in the whole day was when she ran into Scott and he had to get in one last jibe. It had been at the nursing home, she had stopped to hand out bags of lotion and handmade throws she had pieced together from quilting scraps donated by the women's missionary union at the little Baptist church in town. Apparently, Scott had volunteered to play music for the home's Valentine party where they crowned a king and queen from among the elderly residents. She had seen him in the cafeteria area and had hoped to avoid him, but no such luck. "I saw you leaving with Walker last night. Did you give the big boss a roll in the hay? You do realize it was a pity-fuck, don't you?"

Riley hadn't answered; instead she had fled, almost slipping on the damp sidewalk outside. Rushing to the sanctuary of her car, she tried not to think about what the cruel man had said. Seth wasn't like that, what they shared had been beautiful. She knew there wasn't a ring and a promise in their future, but he had wanted her—*her!*—Riley Jacobs. She wasn't a pity-fuck. Tears of doubt rolled down her face and when she returned home and there were no calls or messages on the answering machine, her heart fell. He wasn't going to call. Scott was right.

Trying to put it out of her mind, and continue on with another lonely Valentine's Day, Riley threw herself into her newest project. The Walker family had, almost single-handedly, saved the white egret from extinction.

When the makers of women's hats and plume traders had almost killed off the last beautiful bird for their exquisite plumage, Carl Walker had took it upon himself to build a refuge for them. He had gathered up eight young egrets, raised them in captivity on the island and when fall came, he had released them to fly across the Gulf to South America for the winter. As he had hoped, when spring came, the birds had returned and brought others of their kind and raised their young in the protection of a rookery that he designed and his family maintained to this day. Riley had taken photographs of these birds in all of their glory and had designed and stitched one-of-a kind scenes that could be printed on pillows and tapestries. These could be sold and the funds used for upkeep of the birds and their habitat. As she put the finishing touches on one sample tapestry that she had planned to show the new CEO of Beaucoup, she now realized it would be Seth that she would have to sell this idea to. The realization dampened her enthusiasm.

Staring off into space, she considered what to do. The doorbell made her start, and she put it down to see who was dropping by on a Saturday, perhaps it was Dorothy or Jackie with tales of their conquests from the night before. Instead, Riley was shocked to see a delivery boy standing there with a huge bouquet of red roses. Flowers! She never received flowers! Accepting them with a smile, she tipped the young man and went in to read the card while inhaling their heavenly fragrance. Her heart was hammering, there was only one person that would send her flowers, and that idea was just too wonderful for words. Sure enough, the card read, *"Thank you for everything. I can't wait to see you again."*

Riley turned the card over, but that was all. It was a vague message, a sweet one, but still she couldn't help but wish for more.

About to go put the flowers in some water, another knock at the door caught her by surprise. Reluctant to let go of her beautiful roses, she went back to see who it was. When she opened the door, a smiling Seth stood there looking like a tomcat who had lapped up a dish of cream, and she guessed he had, if you counted the cream that had flowed from her the night before. Just being this close to him had her nipples peaking and her pussy waking up, wanting to be stroked and petted. "Seth! Thank you, so much for the flowers. Please come in?"

Resorting to signing, he told her why he'd come. "It's a beautiful warm day for February. Would you join me for a picnic?" He held out a basket, showing her that it was all packed and ready to go.

Her heart leapt with excitement. "I would love to. Let me put these flowers in water, and I'll be right with you." She looked down at her clothes and decided they were good enough for a stroll and an outing. Blue jeans and a top weren't fancy, but she did have on one of her favorite tops and it made her look slimmer than she usually did. She hurried as fast as she could and didn't resist leaning into the big red blossoms for one last sniff. But her date awaited—wow, what a though—and she couldn't wait to join him. Grabbing her purse, she almost ran back to the door. "I'm ready to go."

* * * *

Seth hadn't been able to stay away. All he could think about was Riley and how her skin had felt beneath his fingers and how sweet her kiss had been. Memories of her climax had haunted him and the rush of joy he had felt when she had sucked his cock would be a gauge by which he measured all other encounters. Funny, he couldn't figure wanting anyone else, but he pushed that thought aside. His life was too full and in too much upheaval to get serious. But still, if he were to get serious, Riley was exactly the kind of woman he would want by his side. She was beautiful, sweet, kind and had a heart big enough to encompass the world. Riley would make any man a wonderful wife. Just not him, yet.

He had borrowed his dad's old pickup that had bench seats and Riley sat close by him while they drove out to the jungle gardens. He knew just the place he wanted to take her. It wouldn't be new to her, but it was beautiful. The park was closed today, and Seth had left strict orders for no island employee to come within a square mile of where he and Riley would be. Today, he was going to make love with this gorgeous woman on a blanket underneath the spreading live oaks where he had played as a child. Coming home was more magical than he had ever hoped for and he owed it, in large part, to the woman at his side.

She seemed to not be bothered by their times of silence. She sat close with her hand on his leg, idly stroking his thigh. His cock was getting harder with every soft caress. With concentrated effort, Seth decided it was time to speak, as best he could. If his broken stammers turned her off, it was better to know now. Biting his tongue, he pushed the words out. "La-la-last night, won–won–wonderful." God, he was sweating in February. Her hand tightened on his leg, encouraging him to go on. "I wa-wa-wa-want to spend ti-ti-time with you." By the time he had struggled to say that sentence his throat was as dry as dust.

Riley gave him her gift of trust. He felt her lay her head on his shoulder, and as she spoke all the doubts he had dissipated. "I want to spend time with you too. I'm ashamed to say that I didn't really expect you to call, and now that you did I am beyond happy." She kissed his arm, through his shirt. "And last night was a dream come true for me, you have to know that."

Bolstered by her admission, Seth grinned with happiness as he turned down the narrow road into the sanctuary. It was an idyllic setting, even in winter. Spanish moss hung thick from the trees giving the whole place a mysterious and eerie beauty. Fields of azaleas were beginning to bud and irises and daffodils were blooming with rampant abundance in every color from deep purple to the lightest yellow. As always, the wild splendor struck him. What his family had built and maintained; this was his legacy, his inheritance. But today, there was something more beautiful at his side, and her quiet, undemanding companionship meant more to him than the stacks of money that lined his family's coffers. He wanted to make love to her, here, in the place they both called home.

"Ca-ca…" He paused to take a breath. "Will you let me ma-ma-make love to you?" The last three words rushed out. It just seemed if she said yes, that he could stand up and deliver a sermon. Riley might just be the secret to his dilemma.

She didn't answer with words, at first; instead she buried her face in his neck and kissed him. "I can hardly wait."

Seth pulled into a small opening in a grove of trees. Gathering Riley, a blanket and the food, he led her to a carpet of moss that would be soft enough to cushion their passion. As he spread the blanket, she gave him a shy smile and started shedding her clothes. "We are alone, aren't we?"

"God, yes," he gruffly agreed, the words seeming to come easier with Riley than with anyone. What he longed to do was make love to her and be able to tell her just what it meant to him. Soon, his clothes lay by hers and he thanked God for the warm dappled sunlight that blessed South Louisiana with temperate weather. Where else could a man make love to his woman out of doors on Valentine's Day? Once again, he was stunned by her beauty. She was magnificently and wonderfully made. Knowing his speech would fail him, still he couldn't resist trying to tell her.

Stepping close enough that her nipples grazed his chest, he whispered, "You are so beautiful. Look at what you do to me?" His cock was fully engorged, throbbing with anticipation and all he wanted to do was sink deep into her hot, wet lushness. Yesterday, his ego had been stroked by her response to him and today he was going to test the chemistry they had and see just how explosive their joining could be.

"Come here." He sank to his knees and drew her down with him. Pushing her to her back, he vowed she wouldn't be cold, he was going to create enough friction and heat to set the swamp ablaze.

"I want to please you," she offered in the sweetest voice. "I'm glad you're my first."

Her announcement stopped him cold, not because it changed his mind, but it sure as hell changed his tactics. Seth had been about to ravish her. He knew how hot she was and he knew she wanted him, but now it was a whole different ball game. Riley was a virgin and deserved his every consideration.

"Oh sugar, I'm glad you told me. You're so precious." Seth set out to show her how precious she was. He showered her face with kisses, captured her mouth and made love to it with his tongue. When she began to moan and gasp, he captured those love noises in his mouth and answered them with groans of his own. With one hand between her legs, he massaged her vulva until it was wet and ready for him. As he played with her clit and her pussy, he sucked at her tits until she was lifting her hips and begging him to make her his.

"Seth, I need you. Please don't make me wait." Her hands were moving restlessly over his body, caressing and kneading. He could feel her little teeth scraping and nipping at his shoulder, she was ready. Rising over her, he looked down at Riley's face. "Take me," she implored. Then in the age old way that women let their men know they were wanted, she opened herself up to him, spread her legs and invited him inside. Taking his cock in his hand, he teased her little slit, making her quiver and gasp.

His gaze was drawn to those tits he loved, as they jumped and bounced with each breath. Licking the nipples, he heightened her arousal before he pushed inside. The tip of his cock breached the tender opening and he kissed her while she hummed her uncertainty. She wanted him but this was new. Riley was untried, untouched, unsullied and by God, she was his. Pushing in, he closed his eyes, relishing the snug glove-like fit enveloping him. *Heaven*! His cock felt like he was sinking deep into warm, slick, soft whipped cream. "Fuck!" he offered up the word like a prayer. "God! This is so damn good!" Words flowed from his lips. Seth had never felt so free.

"More, baby," she urged him. "I want it all." She pushed back a little, begging for a rhythm.

Seth pulled out and then sank back in, deep, deeper than before. He could feel her tighten around him, accepting him. Riley was accepting not only his cock, but his soul, the good, the bad, and the imperfect. Riley was taking him into her body and making him welcome.

It felt too good! He had to move. Seth was getting no resistance from Riley. She wrapped her legs around his hips and her arms around his neck and accepted every thrust with a parry of her own. Granted such freedom, Seth began to pump. He thrust his cock into her over and over, building the heat, making her cream flow. She rolled her head from side to side and dug her nails into his shoulder. Her gasps became faster and she chanted his name, and when her pussy began to vibrate around him—little quivers and spasms—Seth let himself go and he bellowed his climax sending a flock of birds into the air that had been nesting in the trees nearby. The rushing of their wings masked the sweet whimpers and mewls of Riley as she came.

Seth held her close, rolling to one side and hugging her body to his. "Thank you," he whispered. "That was the best Valentine's gift anyone has ever given me." He meant it. She had given him a gift, not only her body, but also the proof that he could be loved and desired despite his handicap.

"You're welcome." She kissed his chest, rubbing her face against his shoulder.

Seth looked over his shoulder at his home. Egret Island and Beaucoup was going to be a challenge in the days ahead. There were changes coming and he would have to decide if he had the will and the wisdom to make his father's dreams come true. But right now there was a more important matter to settle, a question he had forgotten to ask. "Riley, honey," he whispered in her ear. "Would you be my Valentine?"

* * * *

Would she be Seth's Valentine? With a smile and a laugh, she answered, "Yes, I would love to be your Valentine." He had come into her life just when she needed him most. Right now, she had no idea what the future held, or what their relationship would turn out to be, but Seth Walker had given Riley a gift she would never forget. He had shown her that she, Riley Jacobs, was worthy to be loved. She was desirable. She was sexy. Hugging him close, she prayed he would find peace and come to realize what he had to say was so much more important than how he said it.

Would she stay on Egret Island? Well, that question was still to be answered. But right now, she wouldn't have traded one moment of the past two days for anything. "I can't wait to read that author's book, but no matter how erotic her writing is it won't be as good as what we just shared. How about we go back to my place and do it again. I'm still hungry—for you."

"You are?" He nipped at her ear. "How do you want it?"

"How do you think?" she teased him.

And when she breathed the words, *Hot and spicy*, Seth knew he had his work cut out for him. This woman's appetite for loving was just as great as his and he couldn't wait to satisfy her every desire.

The End

Lost in the Sea of You
by
Cynthia Arsuaga

Chapter One

They found the boat in late afternoon, on a February day as cold and dry as any gets in Maine. That's how the adventure began for Mikael Larson, ex-Army, relatively new sheriff and unattached man in a small town. Starting uneventfully at home, by the time he walked into the station, the day turned weird on the way to unexplainable.

The first emergency call logged in mid-morning and the other ten came in rapid succession shortly thereafter. As the newest law enforcement officer on the force, Mikael had taken a lot of grief from the staff the past few months, and thought the calls were another arranged practical joke. One last hurrah before he started reprimanding a few of them. They were really pushing his patience on the jokes. After the most recent call, he decided to play along one more time since today was the *Day of Love* after all. If he didn't put a stop to the incessant calls, the so-called conscientious citizens of Marneport wouldn't cease and would disrupt his well-organized station.

If he ventured to guess who really perpetrated the prank, he'd have imagined mischievous teenagers not the deputies jerking his chain. He'd made his view of such things clear to his employees. Teenagers were another story. Whoever planned the capricious escapade had to show the new southern sheriff in the Yankee village how taking over the position didn't necessarily come with an easy time.

Since Mikael had nothing planned the rest of the day, he snagged the only available deputy, Dennis Valberg, then drove to the location where the mysterious marooned boat rested.

All the reports had been consistent in their description—yellow blistered paint, with a blue pilothouse, a small fishing boat measuring about fifteen to eighteen feet, sitting in the middle of a field. The last part baffled him. The area described was at least a quarter mile from the town's harbor. The storm the night before had been fierce, heavy winds and rain, but to move a small boat far inland would take a tidal wave. Such an occurrence couldn't pass unnoticed, even by a brand new landlubber sheriff.

About an hour after the last call, the two men arrived at the site. Mikael couldn't help but notice how eerie the scene appeared. A fishing vessel set adrift on an ocean of bleak dry tundra.

"Well, will you look at that, Sheriff? Turns out the callers weren't kidding," the deputy commented.

"The vote isn't in yet, Valberg."

Mikael and his deputy exited the black SUV used for official business and walked toward the solitary boat, stepping over dry grass and bog. The blistering February wind bit into his exposed face. *Jesus, Mary and Joseph! Why'd I take a job in Maine in the dead of winter? I could have taken that position in Georgia. It gets cold there, but nothing like this.* At first, leaving Alabama for a new career path in the frigid Northeast in the middle of winter sounded like a good idea, but he made the decision when he interviewed for the job in the mellow days of fall. The leaves were turning, with a pleasant crispness in the air and the town seemed welcoming. After serving ten years in the U.S. Army and most of that in Iraq or Afghanistan, the slower pace of Marneport called to him and something else he couldn't quite explain. He accepted the position before the holidays.

The closer Mikael approached the small vessel, the more the stench from freshly sea-salted decaying seaweed burned his nostrils. Searching the perimeter, he observed no truck marks, footprints or any other evidence as to how the boat arrived. His normal scene assessing instincts kicked in.

"Sheriff, come look," Valberg called out.

As he moved to the aft side, faint writing on the hull caught his eye and he read the name. "Yeah, this is the Helga. Somethin' I'm missing here?"

The deputy nodded. "Yes sir. This old girl went missing about fifty years ago during the Valentine's Day storm of 1962, the worst one of the century."

"You're telling me this hunk of timber has been lost at sea for fifty years and now miraculously shows up? Valberg, do I look like I have stupid written across my forehead. This little boat would be nothing but rotten wood. C'mon fess up, this is another one of you boys *indoctrinating* me 'cause I'm a southern boy in this town, right?"

The young man with dark, short cropped hair pushed his hands into his uniform pants pockets. "No, sir. This really looks like the *Helga*. I've seen pictures. No one ever found her. Became a legend in Marneport as to what happened to her, or so I heard."

"Really? A legend? This little thing. What, the captain go out fishing one day and he got caught in this s*torm of the century*, never returning?"

"Well, yes sir. But, *he* was a *she*."

"Excuse me? A woman as the captain? That must have been an unusual thing fifty years ago."

"From what I know of the story, there was a young woman who went out in search of her lover when the rain began. She took this here boat out against everyone's advice. Not sure what happened after, but a big nor'easter came through and she never returned. Her lover came into port shortly after the *Helga* cleared the harbor buoy. Everyone came to call the story *The Storm-Crossed Lovers*. At least that's the story I've heard. I don't know all the fine details, but that's one of the versions told and more often than not. Kind of sad really."

A pickup truck pulled up alongside the gravel road. The driver exited and walked toward the two law enforcement officers. "Hey, Sheriff, Dennis," the man said, nodding his head to add emphasis to his greeting to both officers. "So do you know who did this?"

"We just got here, Tom. What do you know?" Mikael asked.

"That's what I'd like to find out. This here's my property. I heard the storm last night, lots of wind and rain, but not enough to drop this hunk of junk so far inland. At least not without more help than Mother Nature offered." The baritone voice of the husky man, who stood at least six foot and some, chilled Mikael to the bone more than the surrounding air. The man appeared an intimidating force, and Mikael had heard talk about town that Tom Berger fancied himself as Marneport's honorary Sheriff. Mikael shifted his position.

Mikael met Tom a couple of times, mainly at Tide's Inn and Bar, later discovering he owned the establishment. The tall man had to weigh over three hundred pounds and from what Mikael could tell, liked to intimidate people. As the new sheriff, he'd have to push back or never get respect. Even at his average height of five-ten, he could still bench press and arm wrestle with the best. *Lots of practice in the Army. I can Alpha with the best of them.* He snickered inwardly.

"We're investigating. Are you suggesting you might know who did this?" the sheriff asked, shuffling his feet to stay warm. The wind picked up, penetrating his parka like the proverbial hot knife through butter. He still wasn't used to the cold weather of Maine compared to Alabama's temperate winters.

"Yeah, the punks who came into the bar a couple nights ago did this, I'll bet ya. I had to call you guys to come and run them off. They are from Hammond and nothing but trouble."

"Hmm," Mikael said, glancing at his deputy. "You know anything about this Valberg?"

"I heard Jack and Carl had a call about a small skirmish the other night, but nothing to warrant an arrest."

"I'm telling ya, those boys did this to piss me off. I told them never to come back and then this happens. You going to arrest them, Sheriff?"

"Tom, you want me to arrest the men without justification or proof?" the sheriff asked, getting an acknowledgement from the big man, and then continued. "Do you have the names of these alleged perpetrators? I can't go around arresting people without cause. You can come down to the station and fill out a report and—"

"I'm not wasting my time with your stupid paperwork. I have a business to run. I just want this piece of junk removed from my property. Get them boys to remove it. They put the damned thing here."

The frigid wind bit into the sheriff's exposed face and the civilian was beginning to piss him off. If he didn't think the situation was more than a couple of teenagers' prank, he'd have agreed with the asshole, but in his gut, something didn't seem right. All he wanted to do was get out of the cold and sort this out in the comfort of the station. "Tom, I can't arrest anyone. I see nothing more than an old, small, fishing boat. There's no evidence of foul play or who put this here, correct me if I'm wrong. Once you post a notice, and if no one claims it after thirty days, you can dispose of it anyway you want."

"Thirty days? Are you shittin' me, Sheriff? This is an eyesore. The piece of junk may just find itself a pile of ash. I'm not waitin' thirty days."

Irritation over this man grew. Yes, the wreck of a boat could be considered unsightly, but not so much to warrant this behavior. Mikael took in a deep breath and let it out. *Maintain control.* "You do anything illegal, and I'll throw the book at you. With the dry condition of the ground cover, you torch this boat and there's the risk of igniting a firestorm. I suggest you file a notice, wait the time and have it removed responsibly."

The man grumbled. "So because of a couple punks, I have to spend my time and money to clean up the mess." Then he stormed back to his truck and drove off, the back tires kicking up loose dirt and gravel.

Mikael stared at Valberg. "What the hell is wrong with him?"

"I don't know. He's always grouchy though. So, what do you wanna do, Sheriff?"

"What I'd really like to do—get the frig out of this cold. I don't think there's anything more we can do here. No blood, foul play or any evidence other than this was probably a prank."

"You want me to follow-up with Jack and Carl and see if those boys Tom accused could have something to do with this?"

"Yeah, do that. I don't think this will go anywhere, but at least we can tell Tom we did our job and he can wait the thirty days to dispose of the boat. C'mon let's go. I'm freezing my balls off out here."

A half hour later at the station, Mikael settled in behind his metal and faux wood military-issue type desk to complete the weekly reports. Since the normal workday came to an end around four in the afternoon due to the early sunset he thought he might leave early. Claudia, the office manager and dispatcher had taken the afternoon off. Her husband had plans to take her out for a Valentine's dinner celebration. Before letting her go, Mikael teased and told her she had to stay late to post the reports when he finished. Still chuckling from her joyful reaction, he thought he'd take his own advice and leave too. One advantage to living in a small town and county, the duties as sheriff were minimal. Crime almost didn't exist. The boat incident this afternoon turned out to be the most exciting event since accepting the position of sheriff.

On his way home, he stopped at the grocery store to pick up dinner, all the while kicking the boat incident around in his mind. Something about the entire situation gnawed at his gut. *Helga.* The name seemed familiar. He'd seen the inscription written some place, but where had he seen or heard the name before? He decided the answer would come to him eventually. He never forgot a name or face. Right now he rushed to get back home, turn the cold cuts he bought into dinner and get back to retiling the upstairs bathroom. Turned out the old house he purchased had sat abandoned for years, five to be exact according to the real estate broker. Buying a foreclosure was fortuitous, both financially and physically. He always wanted to renovate an old house, work with his hands and turn something ugly into a piece of beauty. The gratification he received from restoring the old Victorian gave him a sense of belonging to the community and became an outlet to keep his mind off the battle scars of war.

As he approached the front yard, he spied something leaning against the house on the front porch. From the distance, he couldn't make out the person, but whoever they were, they seemed distraught. The night had become darker. The only light came from the street lamp, casting eerie shadows across the figure seated against the clapboard siding.

Is that a package or really a person? His first thoughts were perhaps the package of fixtures he ordered for the bathroom remodel arrived. Then the figure moved. An animal? His mind raced. "What the fuck is it?" he muttered as he picked up the pace. Ever the cautious lawman, he put down the bag of groceries, keeping his eyes on the target. Slowly, he unclipped his gun from the holster approaching in a crouch.

At ten feet away, he focused in on the figure, groaning and slightly moving. He straightened up, stopped abruptly and listened. *A woman?*

Mikael gingerly climbed the three steps to the front porch. The first was quiet. The second one betrayed him with a loud creak. The woman moved, muttering incoherently. She tilted her head up and blinked a few times before speaking.

"Edmond? Is that you?" The softness of her voice brought tightness to Mikael's chest. The sweet sound aroused protective-take-care-of-my-woman urges throughout his now totally alert body.

Moving closer, the face of the woman came into view. He knelt down and as he reached out, she slipped her arms around his shoulders, taking him by surprise. And little ever caught him unaware. He prided himself on anticipating the unexpected, but the swiftness of her move knocked him off balance, mentally and physically. He recovered by pulling back. "Who are you?"

"Oh, Edmond, I thought I'd lost you."

"I'm not—"

Before he could finish, the stranger covered his mouth with hers. The salty and sweet taste burned and excited. His mind reeled. The kiss pressed hard and her tongue tickled, begging for entrance. He wanted to give in, but with a second of sanity, he grabbed her arms and pushed back, releasing the embrace. Before he could speak, her body went limp and she fell unconscious.

Well, fuck. Now what do I do?

Chapter Two

The sliver of early morning light that splintered through the drawn draperies of the bedroom woke Mikael. The night had certainly not been the one he expected to spend. Nothing about yesterday had been normal. A bedraggled strange woman appeared on his doorstep. He assumed she had taken a dip in the ocean, dressed in a tattered cotton dress, wet and smelling of saltwater. A very absurd stunt to pull in the middle of winter off the coast of Maine, he thought. Who would do such an idiotic thing? He had posed this and other questions last night. Unfortunately, she remained unconscious and couldn't answer.

The blasted take-care-of-my-woman testosterone tugged at his insides again as he recalled how he'd removed her wet clothing and gave her a sponge bath, rinsing out the sticky and saltwater tangled hair. Repeatedly, he told himself to look upon her nakedness clinically. *I'm doing this to clean her and make her warm and comfortable.* Yeah, he kept telling himself that over and over. She was a delicate angel who set his blood on fire like the devil, and battered relentlessly at his resolve to remain professional.

For most of the night, he sat beside the bed staring at the mysterious woman in his house. *In my bed.* Before he took his place in the overstuffed chair, he sat on the edge of the mattress raking his eyes over the petite blonde woman. Using honed observation skills, he estimated she was in her early twenties, a baby compared to his thirty-six. He only caught a quick glimpse of her eyes, a chestnut brown with specks of gold. Her breathing slowed and he knew she fell into a deep sleep. The kiss, the intoxicating kiss she gave him before losing consciousness still burned his lips from earlier. Sweet, but salty.

Mikael had pushed his hands into the pockets of his jeans, anything to keep his fingers occupied and away from touching her again. This delicate flower had the softest skin of any woman he'd ever known. Just simple contact with her arms when she'd grabbed and kissed him made his mouth water and fingers itch to handle other parts of her. When he stripped her clothes and gave her a sponge bath, it took every bit of his control not to look too hard. Hard, hell that's what he felt. He slapped himself mentally to get those thoughts out of his mind.

This was Valentine's Day night and he blew off the idea as Cupid playing tricks on him. Tempting him to find love again. But, that's all it was, a fantasy. Loving again was too soon. Not after the breakup with Paula. Maybe four months after a long-term relationship dissolved was more than enough time to get back to dating again for some men, but not him. The so-called love of his life didn't want to follow him to the ends of the earth or even to Maine when he told her his plans to apply for the position. She refused to leave Alabama. "I have friends and family here. I'm not going to some town without a mall and freeze my ass off to boot."

That was the whole crux of the matter in the end. She liked to shop, and shop and shop. The last he heard, she hooked up with a high-powered attorney in Birmingham who could give her everything she wanted. Enough lonely nights had been spent pining for Paula.

As he viewed the angel-on-earth with awe—high cheekbones, straight nose, heart-shaped face—his throat went dry. His ex-girlfriend never looked that beautiful sleeping, or any other woman he bedded, for that matter. Something appealing, seductive and outright helpless had him all twisted inside. Suppressed passion? Him or her? Both? He burned for her and if his growing erection was any indication of how the mere sight of the woman affected him, what would she do awake? Her mouth fell open slightly as she rolled to her side, and it took enormous amounts of self-control not to lean over and kiss her rosy full lips. Time seemed to slow and the image of him stripping her naked again ran through his mind.

He shook off the haze clouding his brain to view the sleeping beauty in his bedroom. He couldn't stop the low groan that shuddered up from his chest as he raked his gaze along the curves of her concealed body. He began to imagine his palms running across her breasts, pausing to rub the pink-tipped nipples until they hardened like pebbles. He wanted her, to caress the curves of her wet and willing body. He imagined dragging his mouth over hers, kissing with passion as his hard cock plundered her soft pussy over and over until they were both hot, sweaty and satisfactorily exhausted.

Damn it! What am I thinking? Disgust hit him square in the face. Had he gone too long without sex that he'd force his attentions on a woman he didn't know? Lusting after a helpless woman sleeping in his bed was crazy. He needed to get out more.

Well damn it, that's what he thought he did by moving to Marneport. Tightening his fists inside the pockets of his jeans, he slipped off the bed and snuggled into the chair to sleep. He had spent the remainder of the night chiding himself for thinking about the woman. Frankly, he'd spent too much time chasing after females who didn't live up to his wants, needs or desires. He had high hopes for the relationship with Paula until everything they had once meant to one another collapsed in a deluge of finger pointing and recrimination. Why he spent one second thinking about her, he didn't know. With one kiss, the cute bundle in his bed made him realize he could move on. Amid a flurry of reassuring thoughts warming his mind, he finally succumbed to the Sandman in the early morning hours.

In the light of day, the memory of the kiss from the night before lingered and still warmed his skin when he awakened. As he glanced over at the slumbering angel who had danced erotically through his dreams, he stretched and readjusted in the club chair pushing against the ottoman his legs rested on. The forced movement caused the round stool to slide across the wood floor making a loud scraping noise. The woman stirred, moaning faintly as she fluttered her eyes open and long, blonde tresses fell across her face.

"Good morning," he said softly.

Obviously startled by his voice, she jerked. "You're not Edmond. Who are you?" She scrunched under the cover, clinging to the bedcoverings tucked under her chin.

Standing, he stepped closer to the bed. "Mikael, Mikael Larson. You're in the bedroom of my house."

"Your house? This is Edmond's house."

The shaking covers made him realize she shivered from fear and not a chill.

"Don't be afraid. I'm not going to hurt you. You were on my front porch when I arrived home last night. What's your name?"

Tears glistened in her eyes as they widened to meet his. "Where's Edmond?"

"I'm sorry, Miss. I don't know who Edmond is. This is my house. I bought it several months ago. I'm the new sheriff in Marneport and I may be new, but I don't remember meeting you before. Do you live around here or in the next town?"

"No, this is my home. I mean, this is Edmond's but Marneport is my home. I don't understand what's happening."

Taking another stride toward the bed, he searched for any apprehension on her part. Seeing none, he sat on the edge of the mattress at the foot of the bed. "I'd like to help since you did end up on my doorstep. Why don't we start with the last thing you remember?"

The expression on her face told him everything. She appeared frightened, confused and not sure to trust him. "It is all right, I won't hurt you. I'm trying to help. Why not start with your name."

Moments passed before she spoke. "Nissa. My name is Nissa Moore."

"Nissa. Pretty name." That nagging feeling tugged at his insides like yesterday. The young woman seemed familiar. He'd seen her before. Where, he had no idea.

"T-thank you."

"Okay, that is a good start. You at least remember your name. Why were you on my front porch, Nissa?" he asked, keeping his voice low and modulated as not to frighten her further.

"I thought I was at Edmond's house."

"Hmm, Edmond again. Who is he? You keep saying this is his house. Maybe in the dark you got it mixed up with another one."

"No! I didn't. This is his house." He could see tears well in her eyes.

"Okay, okay. I didn't mean to push. Where were you? I mean, your clothes were wet and smelled like you had been in the ocean, but I know that is impossible because no one can swim in the frigid water this time of year."

She lifted the coverings and peered under them, then glanced at him with widened eyes. "These aren't my clothes. D-Did you do this?"

The shock on her face had him scurrying for a plausible answer so as not to frighten her more. "Like I said, you were wet and cold and I had to get you out of them before you got pneumonia. I...I didn't look, really. Just removed them fast and put you in one of my college T-shirts." He left out the part about bathing her.

"I'm to really believe you?"

"Yes. I didn't even do anything when you kissed me." The words escaped before he had a chance to retract them.

"Kiss you?"

"Um, not a big deal. You were kind of out of it and you called me Edmond. In your confusion, you must have thought I was him."

She pulled the coverings closer. "Oh. I'm sorry."

"No problem. It didn't bother me." He lied again. "So, did someone hurt you or..."

"No! Just tell me where Edmond is? I have to find him."

"Nissa, I told you I don't know an Edmond." He stood. "Look, I tell you what. I have to go to work today, but under these circumstances I'll stay home. You can stay here, relax, get something to eat, and if you need to shower and clean-up, use the bathroom off my bedroom. The other one I'm renovating and it's not functioning. I'll leave you to your privacy and I'll check on you later. We can figure out what happened to you and find this Edmond when you feel better."

She nodded. He smiled and left the room. A cold shower was needed before he could think of doing any work.

A half hour later he wondered why he bothered with the shower at all. He sat at the desk in his home office shuffling paperwork, trying to forget Nissa Moore. He failed miserably, unable to shake the feeling he recognized her from somewhere. Unusual. Exotic. And oh so damned familiar. Bizarre was all he could say about the nagging thought. He'd called the station an hour before to have Valberg come to the house.

The doorbell chimed.

Mikael opened the door to have his deputy standing before him. "What's up this morning, Sheriff? Why'd you call me over to your house?" Valberg asked, poking his head through the open doorway.

"Valberg, thanks for meeting me here. Come on in, I have a few questions for you."

"Oh, shit. What have I done, boss? You wanted to see me privately. This must be real bad." The deputy walked hesitantly and sat on the sofa in the living area.

Mikael chuckled. "You're not in trouble. I need to ask you about someone I've met. More exact, she showed up on my front porch last night. She's upstairs. Curious thing, she is claiming this house belongs to someone else and can't tell me anything other than her name and she lives in Marneport."

"Whew! I thought I messed up big time. So, you've met someone, huh? You go boss."

"No, I told you it's nothing like that. I need you to run a check on her. See if any missing persons going by the name of Nissa Moore have shown up in any databases. I'd do it, but I don't want to leave her unattended. Nissa is an unusual name and something about her bothered me all night. I was thinking maybe she is related to someone here, maybe used to live in this house and suffered from some kind of trauma."

"Hmm, the name doesn't ring a bell. I haven't lived here all my life, but I do know this house is haunted."

"Haunted. You're kidding, right?"

"Stories I've heard that's all. I don't believe in ghosts. I think the story started because the house had been abandoned for several years. You know how kids can make things up. Maybe this woman is doing the same fishing around for a handout."

"From me? I don't have anything to offer. No, she's pretty convincing. Either she has some form of amnesia or she's a pretty damn good actress. I don't know, but let's see how much information we can find. Let me know, I'll be here all day."

Valberg stood to leave. "Can I meet this Nissa Moore? Maybe if I saw her, I'd recognize her."

"Sure, I don't see why not. She's upstairs in my bedroom."

"Your bedroom?"

"Don't give me that look. It's the only bed I have. Get your mind out of the gutter Valberg. I slept in the chair by the bed."

The two men climbed the stairs to the second floor. Valberg chuckled several times before they reached the landing. "Have you followed up on the boat incident," Mikael asked trying to change the subject.

"There's nothing else I can tell you, Sheriff. The boat was lost at sea during a bad storm fifty years ago. The story goes the woman went out during a storm looking for her boyfriend and never came back. Yesterday, a boat that looks just like the one that went down shows up in an empty field. It's weird, but who knows what really happened."

Mikael shook his head. "Sounds strange I know, but something is not right with the scene. Did you speak with Jack and Carl about the men Tom accused of putting the boat on the vacant property?"

"Yeah, they said no way they did it. They were drunk and not capable of moving a boat that size. And besides, Sheriff, you saw for yourself. No wheel marks, or any other evidence indicating how the boat ended up in the middle of the field. I think Tom is going to have to wait the thirty days to remove the boat, just like you told him."

"Yes he will. Keep an eye on him though. I don't need him to torch it or we'll have a bigger problem."

"I'll take care of letting him know. So which room is she in?"

The two men stood outside a door off the landing.

"Here." Mikael tapped his knuckles against the six-panel wood door. "Nissa, it's Mikael. Can I come in?"

After a few moments without an answer, he turned the knob and pushed the door open.

"Nissa? Are you here? It's Mikael."

"Well, Sheriff, appears your houseguest has left."

The bedcoverings were pushed back, the bathroom door was ajar but no sign of the young woman. He took several strides toward the bed and stopped. "She was here, I swear."

"Maybe this Nissa got her memory back and returned to where she came from."

"I doubt it. Her clothes are still in the dryer downstairs."

"Her clothes? Boy, Sheriff. This story is getting better and better."

"Valberg, this discussion is over. I think it's time to go." Mikael walked to the door and waved the deputy through.

"Okay, okay, if you say so. I'll get back to you about what I find out about this *Nissa*." The snicker by Valberg infuriated Mikael.

Following his deputy, he took one more glance back into the bedroom. Silence and no signs of the young woman. *Where the hell did she go?*

As the two men descended the stairs, Valberg stopped on the last step. "I just remembered. If you want to know more about the boat that went down you can ask Wayne over at Moore's Bait Shop. He's related to the family. The woman who was in your bed might be related. She has the same name and all. Although there are a lot of Moore's in Marneport."

"Old Wayne? I've met him. I'll stop by later."

"Is that it, Sheriff?"

"Yes, for now."

Chapter Three

Where did she go? He wasn't crazy. The woman slept in his bed. He kept a vigilant eye on her all night, barely getting enough sleep himself. This morning she spoke. *How else did I know her name if she didn't tell me? Nissa Moore.*

No way could this be a prank orchestrated by his deputies and staff. If it were, why? Seems like an awful lot of trouble just to jerk his chain, and the woman was no figment of his imagination. He shut the front door and ran up the stairs toward his bedroom.

"Nissa," he called out as he walked around the room. "Answer me. Are you here?"

Peeking into the bathroom, he didn't see her there. Then, he left the room, calling out for her, and walked down the hallway toward the other bedrooms.

"Were you looking for me?" the soft female voice asked from behind.

Startled and angry, he turned on his heel ready to fuss at her for not answering. "Nis…sa," the rest of what he wanted to say couldn't pass his tongue at the sight of her. She stood in nothing but a long sleeved shirt hanging loosely over her petite body with the top three buttons unfastened revealing the swell of her breasts. Her wavy dark blonde hair tumbled loosely over her shoulders. Pale skin enhanced the long legs poking out from under the thigh-length shirt. The full breasts with the rosy hard nipples he remembered rose and fell with harsh breathing and pebbled, poking through the thin fabric. Although he couldn't see the outline, he also recalled the narrow waist that tapered to flared hips.

Familiar, heavy pressure exploded in Mikael's groin. Standing still, he wetted his bottom lip then sucked it between his teeth. The vision of her manifested itself in a picture of innocence. His heart skipped a beat as his dominant-take-care-of-my-woman impulses fired up again. Except unlike last night, he wanted more than to just take care of her. He just wanted to possess.

"That's my name. Don't wear it out," she said coyly, then giggled. "Did you find Edmond for me?"

"I…uh…no, no I didn't." The distance between them shrunk. "Where were you?"

"Oh I thought I'd look around. Did some exploring. I couldn't find Edmond, but I found this." She held up his cell phone. "What is it?"

"My phone," he said matter-of-fact. He grabbed the phone and flipped the cover.

"I thought it looked more like a calculator. I pushed the buttons, but it didn't add up the numbers. Then it started to talk."

"Shit, you probably called someone. Did you answer them?"

"No! I was shocked and dropped it on the floor. I don't think I broke it."

Mikael stepped back, turning and punched in a few numbers. The clicking noises indicated the phone worked, so he closed and shoved it in his jeans pocket. Turning his attention to her, he said, "We need to get your clothes back on you. I washed them and they should be dry."

"Okay. I hope you don't mind me wearing your shirt. The T-shirt was itchy and didn't cover me as much as this does."

Not covering much now. "No, that's all right. Why don't you stay here and I'll get your clothes."

"But I'm hungry. Can I get something to eat?" She stepped closer. The batting of her long lashes and the slight tilt of her head had his cock jumping to life of its own accord, painfully straining against his pants. *Fuck, she's killing me here. Keep control Mikael, keep control.*

Letting out a sigh, he turned and rushed down the stairs, the half-naked woman following on his heels. After he retrieved her clothes, he found her in the kitchen sitting at the small table recessed in the bay window. The expression on her face was one of sadness.

"What's the matter? Are you all right?"

"This isn't Edmond's house." Her head lowered.

"I don't mean to pry, but if I'm going to help you, I have to hear everything. Who is Edmond and what happened to you, Nissa." Placing the dried clothes across one of the wooden ladder back chairs, he sat in another across from her.

"Edmond is my boyfriend. I don't know what happened to me. I remember the storm, the wind and rain was fierce. We had an argument and he left the house. I…I looked for him everywhere and couldn't find him. We were supposed to go out on Valentine's night. Edmond said he had something important to discuss with me, but…everything goes black after that." She glanced up and met his eyes in an intense look. "I remember wandering the streets for hours and didn't find him. I came here and waited. Then…"

"And then, I showed up and you thought I was Edmond."

"Edmond is gone. He gave up on me, didn't he? That's why you won't tell me where he is. You're being gentle and nice because you know the truth."

Mikael reached across the table and touched her arm, rubbing his thumb over her wrist. "Nissa, I don't know. Truly. I told you I'm the sheriff and I can help you find your Edmond, but I need more information. Can you do that for me?"

Through sniffles, she nodded. "Yes."

"What is Edmond's full name?"

"Edmond Fowler. Edmond Daniel Fowler."

"Okay. That's good. I'll call my deputy and see if we can't track him down. When was the last time you saw him?"

"Um, yesterday afternoon. We had lunch at the diner."

"Which diner? Casey's on Brambleton or Stella's Pizza at the harbor?"

"Huh? Neither. The Harbor Breeze Diner."

"That's a new one on me. Where's it at, here in Marneport or Hammond, or…"

"Here in Marneport. Everyone knows Harbor Breeze. It's the only one in the village."

How strange, he thought. Nissa had to be confused. Maybe she suffered from some trauma. She did say she was caught out in the storm. Perhaps she got hit on the head and lost some memory. He'd tread lightly until he found this Edmond Fowler. "Okay let's leave the discussion at that. I'll contact Deputy Valberg and have him work on finding Edmond and in the meantime, I think I promised you something to eat."

"Oh yes, I'm starving. I can't remember the last time I ate. Do you have eggs? I like them scrambled. Oh and toast with jam. I love strawberry."

Mikael chuckled, watching with amusement as a blush began at Nissa's chest and creep up her neck and onto her face. Her innocence made his heart thump hard in his rib cage. He cleared his throat and spoke. "I think I can do that for you. Do you like cheese or any other extras in your scrambled eggs?"

"No, plain and ordinary."

Nothing about Nissa is plain or ordinary. Gorgeous and extraordinary maybe. He smiled and turned his attention to fixing breakfast.

During the lingering feast of scrambled eggs, bacon and toast with strawberry jam, Mikael learned more about the mysterious woman who walked into his life. She grew up in Marneport and worked at the bait shop, but she yearned to see the world. Life in the coastal village was boring, she said. Adventures awaited her on the outskirts of town, she sensed it. The excitement in her face shown brilliantly and Mikael remembered such innocent joy at her age. The ravages of war had all but stripped those feelings from him so for a few stolen moments he basked in her enthusiasm.

Time seemed to have ceased for Mikael, enthralled by Nissa and her stories. Then the shrill ring of the phone startled both of them from the intense conversation. Deputy Valberg had information on the missing Edmond Fowler. The shock of the answer twisted Mikael's insides and raked confusion in his brain.

Hiding his feelings had never been difficult, but he failed at that moment. From the expression on her face, he definitely failed.

"What is it Mikael. Is it Edmond?" She rose abruptly, scooting the chair back with force.

"Yes," he said closing the distance between them. Reaching out to comfort her, he pulled her close against his chest. "I'm sorry, Nissa. He died." *He died years ago, fifteen years to be exact. What the fuck is going on?*

"No, no," she said between sobs. "How? I don't understand."

"Valberg didn't say. He found the records in Bangor. He lived there. Is that where you're from Nissa?"

"Bangor? No, I told you I was born here in Marneport. Why was he in Bangor? This is his house."

"Maybe a summer home?"

"No, I don't think so, but maybe." She rubbed her temples. "I think his parents live in Bangor. I don't know anymore."

Her arms tightened around his waist and his mind raced. How could she be crying over a man dead for fifteen years? From her appearance she didn't look more than twenty-five years old. No, she looked more like twenty-one or twenty-two max. Maybe Valberg had the wrong Edmond Fowler. The possibility existed especially in today's climate of identity theft. Perhaps the man was a fugitive and hiding in Marneport under an assumed name, stealing the real Edmond Fowler's name. *Yes, that has to be it.*

Dizzy with need and the desire to have her, the logical side of his brain told him he shouldn't be feeling this overwhelming need to have her. He barely knew the woman. But what did that matter? He pushed aside the doubts and questions he had about her. Was she crazy? A victim of a crime and the trauma so bad she blocked out the memory and created new ones? At this moment he didn't care. All he wanted was to remain in her embrace, to smell the fresh scent of innocence, to feel her silky skin brush against his, and enjoy the perfect fit of her body enveloped in his. Damn, she was perfect! He wanted her more than he had any other woman in his entire life. The two serious relationships he had, the ex-wife, this had been a big mistake at eighteen, and Paula, who had the most recent tug on his heart, proved he could have a committed relationship.

Nissa raised her chin and stared unflinchingly into his face. Then her eyes widened with shock most likely when she saw the passion burning in his and the slight upturn of his mouth. The lust must have shown through in more ways than from his eyes.

Slowly, Mikael lifted his right hand and brushed her cheek lightly. "You are a beautiful woman and shouldn't be hurt like this," he said softly. "You should feel alive and taken care of. Make love with me."

Nissa gasped. Her mouth parted and she pulled back slightly, but his delicate caress trapped her, leaving her unable to escape.

As she trembled beneath his gentle touch, Mikael cursed silently. Damn it, she'd just found out her lover, imaginary or real, died. Her fantasy lies in ruins. She was frightened, confused and he was taking advantage of her distress. *What the fuck is wrong with me? Stupid! Stupid! Stupid!*

"Y-you want me?"

He traced small whorls on her cheeks, barely touching her skin with his fingertips. "I want to protect you."

Nissa closed her eyes and leaned her head on his chest again. Her breath quickened, and he could feel her nipples pebble hard against him. He slid his hand under her chin and stroked her neck. After a nervous swallow, he trailed his fingers down the length of her arm until he reached her hand. Lifting it to his mouth, he kissed her palm and then cradled it against his chest.

Leaning forward, he brushed her lips with his. Electricity pulsed in the air between them. He plunged his tongue into her mouth. With each dip and stroke, he tasted every tiny bit of her while kneading her soft backside. He ground his cock into her soft belly with slow, rhythmic thrusts. Much to his pleasure, she returned his kiss, her lips pliant but her tongue demanding. It stroked his, performing a frenzied dance in his mouth that took his breath away and made him so hard he wanted to take her right on the kitchen table. Breaking the kiss, he traced his tongue in a gentle line along her jaw and down the side of her neck.

Lifting a hand, Mikael traced her jawline back to her ear where he threaded his fingers through her hair and cupped the back of her head. He pulled her closer, exerting gentle pressure. Lowering his head, he nibbled and nipped her ear and neck until her body relaxed. She shivered beneath his hands, then sighed and turned her mouth to his.

Settling his right hand in the small of her back, Mikael pulled her closer nuzzling and sucking her lips with the passion and ferocity of a man long without a woman.

With a low moan, Nissa opened her mouth, and his tongue swept in to mate with hers in a kiss that became more intense as they tangled in the warm wetness.

She slid her hands upward and clasped them behind his neck.

She wants this too! Mikael cupped her buttocks, lifted her hips, and pressed her rhythmically against his aching erection.

Sighing, she tilted her head as he kissed a passionate wet trail down the side of her neck.

Breaking his kiss, he murmured, "Come with me. I want to do this right. The first time shouldn't be in the kitchen."

She tensed and pulled back. Breathless, she eked out, "I…I can't do this. I'm sorry. I can't do this." Then she turned and ran from the room.

Mikael stood dumbfounded. *Stupid! Stupid! Stupid!* Then he heard the front door open and close. He regained his senses and ran through the kitchen to the porch, calling her name.

Chapter Four

Mikael spent days searching for Nissa. After a week he stopped, accepting she'd left his life the same way she came in, with a whisper and a kiss. Actually, the search stopped, not from finding anything, but because of what he did find. After several days of waiting, he went to meet up with the owner of the bait shop, Wayne Moore the one Valberg told him about. He sat down with the aged man and heard a story that sent shivers up and down his spine.

The woman lost at sea fifty years ago, on Valentine's Day, was named Nissa Moore, his older sister by four years. The boyfriend Edmond Fowler arrived back in port a few hours after she left in search of him. A mild winter rain turned into a violent nor'easter. The small boat and woman were never found. Edmond Fowler pretended to mourn, but Wayne Moore found out the truth months later. The two had an argument over the fact his parents did not want him to marry the small village girl, Nissa. Turned out Edmond Fowler was from a wealthy family and the home in Marneport was a family summer home, one of many. In Wayne's opinion, Edmond used Nissa and when the parents put pressure on him to break off the relationship, he did what they said. Wayne's older sister hinted to him that fateful morning she thought Edmond was going to propose since it was Valentine's. Edmond never returned to Marneport after that day, the house was sold many times, and went into foreclosure about five years ago. No one ever heard from Edmond again. Wayne still blames Edmond and his family for his big sister's death. The venom he spouted surprised Mikael.

The amazing story shocked Mikael even more. Had he hallucinated the entire two days? Did he experience a paranormal phenomenon? Was Valberg's joking suggestion possible? *I don't believe in ghosts.* Then, how could he explain what happened? He touched her, he heard her, and he wiped her tears. And he kissed her. Passionately. And she returned the kiss.

On Valentine's Day he had joked about Cupid intervening in his love life bringing Nissa to his doorstep. Good idea, but he didn't believe in little naked babies flying around shooting arrows at unsuspecting humans either. No, the last week never happened. It was all a dream, a merciless attack on his sleep Mikael couldn't avoid.

Unconsciously, he craved her, though he denied his obsession in the light of day. Nissa's siren call plagued him over the first few months. The angelic face, and eyes the color of soft brown, with flecks of gold like amber, melted his heart. Helpless in his sleep to deny her allure, he tossed restlessly as the image of the woman enthralled him, made his blood burn, creating sparks of flaring need that never really faded.

This woman had become an enchantress, a temptress of unfulfilled desire as he slept. She beckoned to him, calling to him in a seductive whisper winding over his ear, a sultry sound that made him ache and reach for her. The dream was relentless. Night after night he'd take her into his embrace and make passionate love until the early morning hours. Over the long months that followed, her face began to fade and the frequency waned, until all he imagined was a woman of pure make-believe.

As life went on, he plowed headlong into the renovation of his Victorian home, finishing the tile in the guest bathroom, painting, and finally decorating a few more rooms. With the onset of spring, he decided to hit the attic space and clean out the area filled with boxes and crates of discarded items from the previous owner.

Just when he thought he'd put Nissa and the Valentine's Day incident behind him, the pictures and diary he found returned all those feelings. As he sat down to go through the boxed contents, he removed several framed pictures of a woman and man. One of the shots had shown the two standing beside a boat. The *Helga*. Nissa. Edmond? He dropped it in shock and disbelief, shattering the glass. Now he realized why she looked familiar and he recognized the name of the boat. When he purchased the property, he collected all the random items scattered throughout the home, boxed them and put them into the attic until he could go through them at a later date.

This was the later date and he vaguely remembered the picture of the man and woman beside the boat. *Fuck! I saw a ghost, a real apparition of the paranormal kind. Shit! I'm really losing it now.* A shiver ran down his spine. Valberg jested about the house being haunted and he had disregarded his deputy's observation as a joke. But, this wasn't a joke. Mikael didn't feel haunted—no fear, no shaking chains or rattling pictures on the wall or floating apparitions at night since the day she vanished. Or, even before she appeared. What kind of paranormal creature was she?

Over the initial shock, he rummaged through the box to see if he could find anything else explaining who and what happened. Sure, he got the story from Wayne Moore at the bait shop, but there had to be more. He found the more in an old diary written by Edmond dated after February 14, 1962.

After reading the remaining entries in the dim light of the attic space, he swallowed hard and Nissa's story became clear. She was a restless soul searching for her Edmond, except he wasn't alive anymore. She had been jilted and died heartbroken, not in search of him, but because she was upset and sought solace at sea. She died on the small boat during the storm that fateful Valentine's night fifty years ago. They fought over his family and he was cruel to her, but he couldn't go against his parents' wishes. He said hateful things as the only way to rid himself of her. He apologized with an inscription about how sorry he was, but felt she'd get over it. She was young, twenty-two, and would find a nice boy to settle down with, he wrote. He never intended to hurt her. Edmond left and said he'd never return.

But he did hurt her. To death.

Why did she appear now after fifty years? Is the phenomena related to Valentine's Day? Where is she now? If what Mikael experienced was a brief encounter with a woman who was dead because she was denied her lost love, why wait fifty years to come back? To haunt him and seek revenge? She didn't seem the vengeful type. With a kind of left-handed relief he recognized he hadn't seen or heard anything since February of last year. Had she found peace and moved on when Mikael told her Edmond had died? Maybe. He didn't know anymore. The one woman who made his blood boil and head swim appeared to be a ghost.

What am I doing? Lusting after a dead person? "I'm losing it for sure." The only remedy to the situation involved keeping his mind busy. He wrapped up the picture and diary then returned them back to the box. They'd stay in the attic. He couldn't bear to see the items again.

Independence Day came with the annual display of fireworks, followed by Labor Day with a village picnic, then Halloween, and for a few brief moments he hoped the folklore of the dead rising on All Hallows Eve was true. Hell, if she truly were a ghost, wasn't it possible? But no such luck. The remainder of the year's holidays came and went. Work and finishing the last touches of remodeling didn't make his spirit any brighter for the New Year.

As hard as he tried, he couldn't get the image of Nissa from his mind. Their first kiss shared on the front porch continued to burn his lips and the memory of her haunted his dreams. He began to think he was crazy constantly thinking of her. She wasn't a ghost in the truest sense of the word but had the capability of haunting nonetheless. After the first of the year, he went back to the attic and retrieved the picture and diary. He decided he didn't want her presence to fade and kept her picture by his bed to gaze upon her face. Every night, she would be the last thing he saw before sleep and the first thing when he awakened in the morning. He felt like a man possessed.

Weeks later, on a dreary and misty Tuesday morning in February, he dragged himself to the station not feeling like doing much, but after the storm the night before he figured there would be reports of damage and requests for assistance. As it was the staff had been cut due to budget constraints. He pulled extra hours, which was fine with him because work kept his body and mind occupied.

"Morning everyone," Mikael said as he walked in, removing his wool-lined overcoat at the same time.

"Good morning, Sheriff. How are you this lovely Monday morning?" Claudia said with a funny lilt to her voice.

"Morning Claudia. So what's going on? I know that look and that tone in your voice always indicates something's up."

She cleared her throat. "You're not going to believe this." She appeared like she was about to burst with laughter.

"Okay, I'll bite. What?"

"I've gotten—"

"Sheriff, you're not going to believe this!" Deputy Valberg said with uncontrolled excitement as he stormed through the door to the office.

"So, will someone tell me already!"

"I saw it. Just like last time. The same place, the same phone calls, everything." He paused to catch his breath.

Mikael motioned with a shrug of his shoulders. "And, what?"

"The boat, that danged boat that appeared after the storm last year. It's back. And man, oh, man, Tom is pissed. I met him out at the site."

A chill prickled across Mikael's skin. He eyed Claudia, and then noticed the bouquet of five roses with a Mylar red heart balloon dangling from a ribbon on her desk. "Today's Valentine's Day. We had a storm last night."

"Yeah, boss. Identical to last year. Weird, eh? I think we've got a serial prankster on our hands." The deputy snickered.

"Not likely, but you have an idea there. So Old Tom was pissed? I thought he got rid of the boat last time. What happened, someone find the old wreck again and put it back out there on the lot to tick him off?"

"I don't know, but he claimed the boat disappeared a few days later last time. All this time, he assumed we found the perpetrator and had the person remove it. I told him we assumed he did. Isn't this the weirdest shit you've ever heard?" He paused and glanced at the dispatcher. "Sorry about that Claudia."

Mikael's mind raced. He forgot about the *Helga* since he never heard from Tom Berger again. Even when he found the diary and Nissa's picture. All the pieces were falling into place and he had a gut feeling he had to act on.

Without hesitation, he hurried out the office. As he reached the door, he peered over his shoulder and said, "I forgot something at home. If it's an emergency Claudia, call me. Otherwise, I'll be out most of the day." If his hunch was correct, he had no intentions of coming back at all. In fifteen minutes, he'd know for sure.

As he approached the house, he spied someone slouched on the front porch. *Déjà vu?* The figure was her, he knew it, and every bone in his body said she was there. Just like the first time he found her. His Nissa.

Mikael's heart stalled when he realized his missing lover had returned and at that moment he didn't know what to say. "Nissa, are you really a ghost? You're dead, aren't you? Should I care? Where did you disappear to?" he muttered one question after another as if practicing. God only knew how long he rehearsed the scene over and over in his head if ever he had the chance to see her again. If this was a dream or she enchanted him somehow, so be it. Here she was, waiting for him as she did before, the only difference he didn't find her until night. That day a year ago she must have waited the whole day. This time would be different all the way around. *If I'm crazy seeing a ghost of a woman dead for fifty years, let me have her before they lock me away.*

Mikael kept focused on her as he closed the distance in double-time. When he was within a few feet, she stood and a smile lit up her face. Climbing the three risers to the front porch, he never took his eyes off hers. He held his breath as he used slow deliberate steps to approach her the last few feet. Soon he stood within inches, those piercing amber-brown eyes unnerved him as she pouted. She glowed from the sunlight hitting her moistened skin. Suddenly, he realized she was wet and shivering in the cold air.

Mikael took her hands and tucked them inside his jacket to warm them. He wanted her to experience the feel of his warmth, his beating heart, his desire for her body and know he was alive waiting for her to be the same, if only in a dream.

"Hi Mikael, I've been waiting for you." She tilted her head up and blinked a few times before speaking again. "I returned for you. I realized I belong here, with you, not Edmond. Isn't that weird? I want you, Mikael." Nissa moved her hands from his chest and wrapped her arms around his neck, slithering her body against his. She fingered his hair at the nape of his neck and gently caressed him with her fingertips.

"Nissa," he whispered.

The sweet voice he thought he'd never hear again quickened his breathing and his heart to race. Those dominant-take-care-of-my-woman impulses firing on all cylinders through his tense body clicked on again. "Nissa," he repeated in a whisper, succulent lips pursed. "I thought I'd lost you." *Oh yes, I'm certifiable. Absolutely certifiably crazy.*

"No. You wanted me and I heard you calling. I was frightened when you kissed me, but now I know I shouldn't be afraid. You said you wouldn't hurt me. I believe you."

Her statement took him by surprise. *I frightened her last time? She heard me calling?* Nothing mattered, she was here and how or why made no difference in the end. He had dreamed of touching her again, kissing her sweet lips and before she had a chance to object and disappear again, he lowered his lips to her mouth. Exploring the shape, the salty taste, the heat of her mouth, he coaxed her lips open swiping his tongue along the seam of her mouth. She mewed and arched toward him, wanting more. He wanted more. If she truly was a ghost, he didn't care. He felt her beneath his touch and wanted to have her beneath him in bed.

With a groan, her mouth opened. Hesitation faded and her lips softened. The kiss deepened. He invaded with his tongue, tangling with hers in a passionate dance, consuming her until she was breathless. The bitter salty flavor of her mouth mingled with his. Surges of pleasure skittered along his skin, sending his cock pulsing with need.

He stroked both of his hands down her back, along her spine, until he cupped her ass. Pressing his fingers into her buttocks, he groaned and slowed down. He pulled back. *What a welcome home!* His cock swelled and his balls tightened. Hell, more than that, he needed to come. How long had he wanted this woman? A year? And the kiss, not an ordinary "happy to see you kiss", but an oral assault and he wanted more. He wanted to fuck her—right now, but making love to Nissa on the front porch, in the February winter air, was not a smooth move. He reached in his pocket and pulled out the house keys and unlocked the front door.

"We need to continue this inside."

Sweeping her into his arms, Mikael carried her through the threshold, ascended the stairs and into his bedroom. He lowered her to the floor, and then proceeded to remove the tattered wet clothing all the while placing feathery kisses along the exposed flesh.

When she stood before him naked, he kicked off his shoes and quickly dropped his trousers and shorts in one fast swoop. Partially unbuttoning his uniform shirt, he pulled it over his head. He grabbed her hand and led her into the bathroom. "We need to clean you up and get you warm. You're shivering."

Chapter Five

The hot, steamy water softly flowed down their bodies from the rain-style showerhead. Mikael eased her petite body between his taut form and the running water. She closed her eyes, and he could see her muscles relax, warming to the sensation of the water dancing over her skin.

Mikael reached for the shampoo and lathered the fragrant mixture into her long blonde tresses. The coconut scent reminded him of the last vacation he had in St. Thomas with Paula. *Shit! I don't want to think of her. Only Nissa.* How he missed his mystery woman. How could she be a figment of his imagination, or a ghost? She was real flesh under his hands. If this wasn't happening right now and was just only another one of his dreams he had over the past year, then don't ever let him awaken from the exquisite manifestation of his mind.

He rinsed the shampoo from her hair. Using the washcloth to gently scrub her body, he relished the pleasure he took from caring for her needs.

Stowing the terry cloth, he washed her using his hands, running them over her soft body. Closing his eyes, he glided the tips of his fingers almost reverently across every inch of her skin. Lightly caressing along a firm back, down a flat belly, and over the tops of her thighs.

"You are so beautiful, Nissa," he whispered in her ear.

He turned her and slid his hands over her back, and then gently kneaded from her shoulders to the curve of her buttocks. A soft moan escaped, deep in her throat. Nissa surrendered to his caress as he felt her body relax into his.

Lathered in creamy soap, Mikael eagerly splayed his large hands over her soft, voluptuous breasts, massaging them. He teased her nipples, tugging and squeezing them. The foam ran down over her body from his deliberate, provocative vexing, making its way over her stomach and hips. Bracing against the tiled wall, she spread her legs exposing a slick wet pussy to his hands. Gliding along her wet slit with two fingers, he then dipped them inside. He toyed with her clit with his thumb, while maintaining his fondling hold on her breasts.

Mikael caressed her bare skin from behind, the water streaming down too sensual for them to withstand without reacting. The back of her head came to rest on his chest gently, the water from the showerhead continuing to cascade over them.

Slipping between her inner thighs, he stroked the erogenous flesh with soap-filled hands. With a light touch of his fingertips, he brushed along her wet folds. She moaned and he couldn't wait much longer. He bent over and leisurely licked her hot, wet slit before continuing down the insides of her legs.

Mikael massaged her calves and thighs, working toward her pussy before he lowered his mouth to her soft flesh, using a firm tongue to lick her hot, wet slit. When she moaned again, he drove his tongue into her. She arched against him, and he sucked on her clit, nibbling and tugging on the sensitive button until he felt her quivering and knew she grew close to her peak. As he touched her lips, the softness of her body pressed against him and he sensed her body relaxing into his as he pulled her tight. He worked magic using his hands and tongue, gliding over every inch of her body.

With one of his hands, he stroked along her warm, sopping wet folds. Slowly, he entered her with one finger, then two, pumping in and out. "Come for me, sweetheart," he whispered.

"Oh yes, Mikael. I'm coming."

Lowering his mouth to her pussy, he licked at her slit and slipped his tongue inside her sex. He stimulated her clit with his thumb then captured her clitoris in his mouth, sucking and nibbling. Alternating between plunging into her pussy and tugging at her tight little nub, he slipped his fingers in and out in a rhythmic motion awaiting her cries of satisfaction. Hissing, her breath passed between clenched teeth making sounds part rapturous and part feral as her body went taut. When the wave of the orgasm was over, Nissa leaned forward, resting on his shoulders to catch her breath.

With exquisite care, he guided the water over her hair and back to remove the last bit of soap before shutting the water off. Grabbing a couple of white towels, he stepped out of the shower, placed one around his waist and used the other to dry his beloved.

He scooped her into his arms after toweling her off, and carefully walked to the bedroom. Laying her on the mattress, he stretched out beside her before his mouth captured hers and his hands began their quest to know her body intimately. He left hers lips, trailing hot kisses across her neck and collarbone until he reached her breasts. Once there, he licked and sucked first one then the other, until she whimpered with desire. Sliding his fingers between her thighs to play in the slippery folds, he parted her cleft with his thumb. He skimmed his index finger over her swollen and sensitive nub.

When she thrust her hips against his hand, he began a slow, circular motion. He smiled against her nipple, feeling her moist folds contract around his fingertips. She tugged at his damp hair.

Mikael reveled in her passion and gave in to his own.

"You are so soft," he whispered, bending his head and rubbing the fleshy side of her breast with his cheek. "Warm and filled with life."

"Y-yes," she stammered. "Of course I'm alive."

A lump gathered in his throat. He realized in the back of his mind she wasn't alive. She died fifty years ago, but she believed she was alive. He didn't know why this was happening. All he believed at that moment was what he could feel and see. She was real and alive. He put the thought out of his mind and concentrated on following his dream into insanity.

Her hands skimmed down his body and brushed against his erection. Then she caressed the hard length of him. He raised his head, locking his eyes on hers. He dropped a hand, running it under her thigh and lifted, then leaned over and captured her mouth.

He held her thigh over his hip and felt her gasp against his lips as he pressed his crotch to hers. Releasing her mouth and leg, he returned his attention to the white skin between her breasts, loving the whimpers she made. He traced kisses from one taut nipple then the other, teasing the erect buds with light flicks of his tongue until she grasped his hair.

"Please! Mikael I need you inside me."

Mikael lifted his head. "Not yet." Then he reached down, spanning her waist with his hands and drew them slowly over her smooth pale skin.

He cupped her breasts in his hands, relishing their fullness and their response as her nipples beaded. *Definitely not finished playing here yet.*

When he captured one of the hard peaks, she cried out and thrust her hips against him. Her silent pleas for penetration only encouraged him to tug harder, drawing moans of enjoyment from her. He pressed his long, hard cock against her pelvis to tease her pussy. The foreplay and chemistry was incredible, and he wanted to extend the pleasure as long as he could maintain control of his own desire.

Releasing her breast, he seized her firmly by the hips and slid both hands down the outside of her thighs, trailing kisses down her belly until he reached her pussy. She cupped her breasts, caressing and squeezing, while he teased his tongue over her wet folds, licking her juices and then sucking on her clit, hard.

Mikael relished her delicious taste—the tangy, yet slightly salty nectar. Nissa sobbed his name as he took his time exploring her. He kept a firm hold on her thighs as she bucked beneath his mouth, her cries getting higher and more breathless while he teased his tongue in and out, alternating between her clit and cunt. He lapped up the juices that flowed, pushing his tongue in as deep as possible.

Plunging a finger, then two into her dripping wet slit, he stretched her moist walls. She thrashed beneath him, meeting every thrust inside.

"You're so fucking tight, Nissa," he growled as he slid a third finger in and pressed firmly against her G-spot.

Nissa arched her hips as she cried out his name.

"Fuck, you're an enchantress that's bedeviled me. Come for me, Nissa." His voice was husky, filled with his own need to pleasure her first. He continued his rhythmic rocking of his fingers inside her, her hips keeping time with him. Cries of delight slipped out of her gorgeous mouth as her release swept over her. Her inner muscles clamped down on his fingers, squeezing hard. As she came down, he slowly calmed his movement before easing his hand away. He traced his dripping fingers down and over her, flitting over her back entrance, curious to see her reaction. When he didn't get any adverse response, he lightly pressed one finger against the tight hole, circling in a gentle and delicate touch. At first she flinched in reaction to his intrusion, but soon relaxed, moaning softly.

Mikael watched in breathless anticipation as she arched up and slowly pressed herself against his finger.

When she slid one hand down to her clit and began to rub, then slipped a couple fingers from her free hand into her pussy, urgency spiked through him. The seductive act relaxed the muscles in her ass allowing Mikael to ease another finger in, massaging the tight forbidden passage. The sight made his erection even harder, if that was possible. He was quickly losing control, unable to hold on much longer. The urge to take her now, fucking her senseless was damn strong.

"Mikael," she barely eked out in a breathless moan that revealed her approaching climax. "Please, I need you in me now."

Keeping his fingers tight in her ass, he leaned over her, kissing the pouty mouth, then sucked on her bottom lip, drawing it between his teeth. He released the kiss, withdrew his fingers from her ass and pushed her thighs wider with his knees. Her sable brown eyes widened and the pupils dilated, as she bit her bottom lip. The look made his cock quiver against her belly.

She pushed her hips upward. "Now, Mikael. Please."

Taking a deep breath, slowly letting it out, he growled deep in his chest. His head was swimming from the rush of sensations. He'd shifted his hands and lowered to his elbows on either side of her. He leaned over and kissed her roughly, thrusting his tongue in her mouth so she could taste herself as he eased the tip of his steely shaft into her wet sheath.

As he slowly pressed into her slippery opening, she gasped into his mouth. He thrust deep then pulled out, then in again stretching her one delicious inch at a time until his balls rested against her. As she squeezed her muscles around him, Mikael gripped her hips, angling her opening for greater penetration. Breathing hard, he stayed still for a moment, allowing her to adjust to his size. He reached forward, tracing his fingers up the sides of her body and cupped her breasts. She trembled beneath him from the sensation.

He drew back and released one of her breasts. As he slid his hand under her ass, he lifted her to plunge deeper. She moaned as he eased his thick shaft in to impale her fully from the new angle. He went to draw back and she moaned, wrapping her legs around his waist. He drew back slowly, and then eased forward again. Getting a tighter grip on her hip, Mikael began to fuck her with long, hard strokes, keeping the pace steady while at the same time pushing his thumb into her ass.

Her eyes drifted closed and her breaths came in uneven, small bursts. "Mikael, I'm coming." Clinging to his shoulders as his thighs slammed into her, she let out a guttural shriek of pleasure.

Back and forward, in and out, he stroked his rock-hard cock and she tightened her inner muscles around his hardness.

Pulling out almost to the point where his cock would pull free, and then thrusting forward again, he plunged deep and fast with each succession. Mikael ran his thumb over her clit, causing Nissa to buck and grind her hips uncontrollably against him. Every nerve ending sparked electricity from the sensation of her wailing orgasm as the adrenaline rush exploded and mind-shattering joy rippled through him.

"That's it baby," he coaxed with a husky tone of voice. "Keep creaming on my cock. Give it to me. Come for me, Nissa."

Intense spasms erupted as she climaxed, her inner muscles pressing around his cock, milking him to an orgasm. He increased the speed of each thrust until moments later he reached his peak.

"Ahhh, fuck, Nissa," he growled as a mind-numbing orgasm ripped through his body, his hips clenching in release. As he expelled his seed deep inside her hot pulsating cunt, his body trembled. A hiss of air escaped through clenched teeth as he slowed his pace, and then collapsed on top of her. The carnal passion was raw, animalistic, wickedly so unbelievable, he'd never experienced such an explosive feeling in his body, or heart. He sensed she never had either.

Caressing her face with tender strokes, he slanted his mouth over hers and kissed her passionately. If this were a dream, he'd be happy for the rest of his life, right here, right now, never wanting to wake up.

They made love three more times, through the afternoon, into evening and the last time in the early hours of morning before falling blissfully asleep, fully exhausted and sated.

The next morning, he awakened early. He glanced over and saw Nissa still sound asleep. His heart thumped hard, his first thoughts were that he did dream making love with her. Brushing the long tresses back from her face, he leaned over and kissed her cheek. He smiled a contented smile. Falling in love shouldn't be this easy, so profound, so fast. But, it was as if he'd known her all his life, waiting for her to come into it. *If this is insanity, call me certifiable. No way she's a ghost. She's a hot, breathing, sexy woman. There has to be some explanation. She has to be related to the first Nissa Moore.*

Rising from the bed, he pulled on a pair of jeans and slipped on a T-shirt and quietly stepped out of the room. He was starving and sure she would be when she awakened. They had been so wrapped up in their passions yesterday; they barely ate enough to keep up their energy. He decided he'd fix her favorite—scrambled eggs, bacon and toast with strawberry jam. And a large pot of coffee!

When he returned to the bedroom and opened the door carrying the tray with the food, she was standing with her back to him.

"Well good morning, sleepyhead," he said cheerfully as he placed the tray on the bed.

"Nissa, are you all right?" he asked when she had not turned to respond to his greeting.

Something on the floor, at her feet, caught his eye. *Shit! The diary!*

She slowly turned to face him and he spied the picture of her and Edmond by the boat clenched in her hands. He noticed tears trickling from her eyes onto her cheeks. Raising her head, the frame slowly slipped from her grasp and crashed on the floor. "I'm dead. I remember everything."

The phone rang. He ignored it. With a couple quick strides he was before her, wrapping his arms around her.

The phone rang again.

His embrace began to collapse in, her body became translucent.

"Nissa, no. Come back to me," he cried out. "I love you."

The phone rang again as he stood watching her visage disappear before his eyes.

Before the last of her faded, she spoke in a distant voice, "I love you Mikael. I will return. Wait for…"

And then she vanished from view. He was alone and the phone rang again, this time he answered.

"What!"

"Sheriff? It's Valberg. You okay?"

"Sorry. Yes. No. What is it, deputy?"

"Tom Berger did it, just like he said he would. He torched that damned boat and now we have a runaway fire on our hands. The fire department is working on getting it under control. I have Tom under arrest. Did I do the right thing, boss?"

"The boat? He burned it? Is anything left of it?"

"No, went up like matchwood along with all the dry grass it sat on."

"She's gone and there's no way for her to come back," Mikael murmured.

"What boss? Who isn't coming back? The *Helga*? I don't think so. She's nothing but a pile of charred wood and ash. She's never coming back."

Chapter Six

He woke in a cold sweat with his heart beating furiously. It happened every time Valentine's Day drew near. The dream became more real, more intense during that time. His mind whirled, wondering if this February the fourteenth would be the year she returned. Every year for the past five he had waited for Nissa, but she never did return.

Alone, in the Victorian home he finished remodeling three years ago, he settled into his position as Sheriff of Marneport and life became very easy. There was pain, an immense amount in the beginning when Nissa faded from his life, but over the years he adjusted. He spent the first couple years researching paranormal phenomena, and even hired a psychic at one point to help him communicate with the dead in hopes of contacting Nissa. That turned out to be a waste.

During his waking moments, Mikael knew his life would never be the same. He carried an enormous weight of anger and resentment at circumstances he couldn't control. The woman he loved was dead; the woman he made love to had been alive for those few brief hours. The memory would sustain him the rest of his life. A life taken away in the uncontrollable blink of an eye the second he had given his heart to her, and she'd disappeared taking that broken heart to wherever dead ghosts go. He had discussed that issue with the psychic in detail. Where do ghosts live? Somewhere in-between life and death? The psychic told him Nissa had unfinished business on this plane of existence, whatever the hell that meant. He was a logical thinking man, one that believed in what he could perceive with all his senses. To him, Nissa had been alive, not dead. His mind kept reliving each touch, kiss, and embrace. Every move he made, every misstep along the way, he'd regret leaving that photo and diary for her to find for the rest of his life.

Finally, after five years of no reappearance, he gave up knowing all he'd ever have would be the memories of a kiss that tasted like the sea on her lips, the surrender of her body, and being lost forever in her heart. He'd be content with that.

Today, he made the decision to move on, but knowing he'd never be able to love another, he'd put all his love and energy into work.

* * * *

"What day is it, Sherry?" the old man said, peering through rheumy eyes at the home health nurse.

"Mister Larson," the woman's voice breached a tone of motherly chiding, "I told you earlier. It's the fourteenth, Valentine's Day to be exact." She cocked her head and gave the patient a small smile. "Are you expecting something today? A valentine gift, perhaps? You know you can't have chocolate or anything sweet."

"I don't want candy. I wanted to know what day it was. Did it storm last night?" With the tips of his trembling and contorted fingers, he fidgeted along the light blanket covering his frail body. "Cranky old woman," he murmured.

"I heard that. Yes, we had a storm last night. A bad one. Now, you behave. My shift is almost over and your day nurse will be here any moment. Don't be giving her a hard time either. I understand she is new with you. Alice took the day off to be with her husband for Valentine's Day."

"Ah, another one I have to break in."

The nurse chuckled. "You're too much. Now rest, I'll get your breakfast." She turned to leave and he grabbed her wrist.

"No." He struggled to get the word out. "Don't leave me." Gasping for more air to continue, his grip tightened. "I'm going today. She's coming for me."

Placing her hand over his, she smiled and gently pulled from his embrace. "Mister Larson, you're not going anywhere. Now, rest. I'll be right back with your breakfast."

The doorbell chimed, three baritone dongs followed by two quick high pitched tings.

"Ah, that must be your day nurse." Nurse Sherry waddled off to answer the door. As she passed the bedroom door, she glanced over her shoulder to her patient and shook her head. "The old coot is losing it. Probably not long now," she whispered walking away.

A few minutes later, she returned accompanied by the day nurse.

Keeping her voice low, she spoke with the new nurse. "I know this is your first day with Mister Larson. He's not a real problem. Just maintain his pain meds and fluids. I have his breakfast ready on the stove, although he appears to be sleeping now. A few minutes ago he was grabbing my wrist and asking what day it was. The man is slipping fast, but he is eighty-six years old and has terminal cancer. I gave him his meds last at six and he won't need another dose for a couple more hours. You can find any other instructions in the journal here." Nurse Sherry pointed to the notebook on the dresser against the far wall of the twelve by twelve bedroom. "If you run into any problems, but I'm sure you won't, you know to call the office."

"I'll be fine. Mister Larson is in good hands with me. You have a good day."

The off-going nurse picked up her heavy wool coat slung across the upholstered chair, her tote bag and paperback book and departed.

The young woman smiled and then glanced down at the older man. The gray hair on his head spiked in every direction. The lines on his face were deep and long, furrowing along his brow and around his eyes. His skin appeared translucent and thin, the pure shade of newly fallen snow. She sensed the flow of blood through the pale blue veins and watched the labored rise and fall of his ribs. The minutes ticked by as her breathing synchronized with his. Gradually, his breaths slowed. Then, they ceased.

An instant later, a brilliant light burst through the closed door of the bedroom. The elderly man's eyes popped open and glanced toward the woman standing beside the bed.

"You finally came back, Nissa."

A smile stretched across her angelic visage. "Yes, Mikael. You waited for me. I said I would return for you." She outstretched her arm, presenting an upturned palmed hand. "Come, my love. It is time to go."

Mikael pushed himself up into a sitting position. Locking his eyes on the vision before him, he became aware of the fact that his body was youthful, virile. The infirmities of age had fallen away. Trying to understand what just happened, he closed his eyes and then opened them again. He examined the new young him.

The woman laughed. "Don't worry, Mikael, it's still you."

Taking in a deep breath, he placed a hand in the beautiful young woman's before him, smiling as he did so.

"Come, we have much to celebrate this Valentine's Day, Mikael."

"You took so long to return, Nissa."

"Fifty years is less than the blink of an eye in the face of eternity."

As they walked toward the light, Mikael glanced over his shoulder at the shell of what used to be his body lying upon the hospital bed. Turning back, he focused on the woman in his embrace. "I love you, Nissa."

"And I you, Mikael. Now and forever, always.

THE END

Cupid's Target
By
Dana Littlejohn

Chapter One

April Harding never considered herself a winter person. She didn't like anything about the season. The wind was cold and cruel as it wreaked havoc on her skin and nails. The clothes you had to wear were heavy and usually dark and dreary. It was darker earlier and the bills were higher because you had to turn on the lights sooner and crank the heat to keep yourself warm.

It was one of the coldest days they'd had in weeks. Against her better judgment, April had bundled herself up to brave the elements as a light snowfall attempted to dust her car. While she should be at home warming her frozen body by the fireplace, she was in fact on her way to the mall pondering what to wear to a Valentine's Day party. She usually made it a priority to go out only to work or get food during this time of the year, successfully hibernating while waiting for spring thaw to occur impatiently, but those plans had been altered.

"You can't tell me that this isn't one of his most ludicrous ideas to date," she grumbled.

"Now April, you only think that because it's cold and you have to be out in it. If Mr. Bowman had suggested this in June you wouldn't have a problem with it at all," a female voice chastised in her ear.

"You are absolutely right, Margot. If it were June I wouldn't have a problem with it. Driving would be easier, walking around searching for the right outfit would be much more pleasant and getting off early to do all that would be great, but it's freaking February. When it's a million degrees below zero out here it kind of sucks the fun out of shopping."

Margot giggled. "Okay, I'll give you that. I know it's a business function, but try to make the best out of it. It's still a party, you know. Good food, free drinks, dancing…you know, a party."

April sputtered. "I'm sorry, I don't recognize those words put together in that capacity."

Margot laughed as April turned the corner. April scanned the frozen looking parking lot for an open spot and clicked her teeth.

"You should see this parking lot, Margot. It's crazy out here. It's not even rush hour yet. Did everybody get off early to go to the mall?"

"Well, Valentine's Day is tomorrow, April. Those are most likely the last minute shoppers you're running into."

April scoffed. Just like her boss decided they would attend the meet and greet downtown with several other visiting company at the last minute.

"I have no business at this party," she told her friend.

"Someone has to be there to represent the company," Margot reminded her.

April spied an opening and headed for it. "Why can't the old man go by himself?"

Margot laughed again and she knew why. Mr. Bowman was more interested in the party part of the business functions they attended. He paid her and Margot very well because their knowledge of the company was extensive. They handled the work end of things.

"Okay, okay, I guess I knew better than that," she said unable to stop her own titters from escaping. "You could have done this one for me, you know."

"Uh-uh, it's your turn. Besides, I have taken one for you."

"What? When did you—"

"Oh, you're going to tell me you don't remember last year in Chicago?" her friend asked, a sharp edge to her tone.

April giggled. She remembered. Spotless Cleaners was meeting with the reps from Gleaming Shine window cleaner. Roger Wilcox gave the presentation. He was very knowledgeable about the product and they ended up buying, but he was the most obnoxious man they had ever met.

April had begged Margot to go to the party because she had a boyfriend and Roger would have to back down with that knowledge.

"That man harassed me all night with his ridiculous 'what happens in Chicago stays in Chicago' line."

April laughed. She could almost see Margot rolling her eyes at the memory.

"I had to pretend to be on my phone the whole time just so I could ignore him and still be politically correct."

"Oh all right. Maybe I'll be able to get through the night and win the client over without meeting anyone significant."

"Good luck with that."

April chuckled again, then sighed. "All right, Margot. I'm here."

"Okay. Send me a picture of the dress you pick."

"I will. See you Monday."

April pushed a button on the device in her ear to disconnect the call. She took a moment to don her gloves, then pulled her hat from the passenger seat onto her head before leaving the car. Crunching across the packed snow in the parking lot, she hurried into the store.

Familiar with the mall's surroundings, she went straight to Sexy for all Seasons. Moving directly to the winter line, April encountered several pretty dresses on the racks in her size, but she flipped through them with a frown on her face. She really had no business at a Valentine's Day party, work related or not. That kind of thing was for people with significant others and unfortunately she hadn't had a lover in a long time.

April finished jerking the dresses along one rack not really looking at them and moved to the next fuming over her situation. She continued yanking one after another not expecting it, but determined to find something because her boss was paying for it. With a huff, she walked through the store glancing at different displays, clearance shelves and stands when a blur of gold caught her eye. Slowly April retraced her steps and turned to a bracket she hadn't inspected. Pushing a few dresses to the side, the perfect outfit came into view. She smiled and lifted it to her body.

"Well, if I have to be tortured at this thing at least I'll look good enduring it." April made it home close to six o'clock. She hurried to make something to eat and rushed a shower. Her food was too hot to eat after she got out, so she left it on the table to cool as she did her hair and makeup. When she was done, April checked her dinner again and it was too cold. Frustrated and pushed for time, she left the food in the microwave and went to get dressed. Still hungry, she grabbed two slice of bread from the top of the refrigerator, stuffed them into her mouth and put her shoes on.

Stumbling around the room, she gathered the rest of her outerwear as she ate the bread. She snatched her coat from the closet and rushed out the door.

Chapter Two

At the Radisson, several companies took advantage of the holiday, to party and meet potential clients for their businesses. Grant Murphy, Gregory Thomas and Daniel Robbins were inside the overcrowded, noisy Continental Ballroom.

"I hate these dumb parties. What kind of business party has a Valentine's Day theme?"

"Well Greg, like most people in this town, they don't need a reason to throw a party, but when one comes around they take full advantage of it," Grant answered him with a laugh in his voice. "It was time to get together to expand our possibilities and make new connections. Valentine's Day just happened to be the next holiday on the calendar," he added with a shrug.

"Well, I don't mind at all. I brought my wife and we're having a good time and I get to take care of business too," Daniel said lightly, waving to a woman across the room.

Grant chuckled. "I kind of like the idea that someone has put a day to the side once a year to remind us to take the time and to do something special with our sweethearts." He patted Daniel on the back and chuckled. "Valentine's Day can only get better once you hook up with someone you love. We all hope to be as happy as you and your wife are some day."

Greg sputtered. "Speak for yourself."

Grant and Daniel laughed at their friend, then clicked their glasses together. As Grant took a sip of his drink, he spied what he suspected was a woman dressed almost like an Eskimo at the door peering inside the conference room. His curiosity was piqued as he watched her emerge from her coverings.

She pulled her gloves off revealing dainty, soft looking hands. Next, she unraveled the scarf from her head and neck exposing her lovely face. Her sensual and luscious, full lips were tinted burgundy making them stand out from her smooth mocha complexion. Grant's glass stopped halfway to his mouth when he tried to take another sip of his drink. His conversation with his friends ended. Their voices faded behind him as he took a step forward, focusing in on her.

Grant continued to watch with bated breath as the woman unwrapped herself like the Christmas present he wished he'd gotten. Slowly, she undid each of the buttons on her long brown coat. When full view of her curvaceous body, seductively adorned in a long black dress trimmed in gold was revealed to him, Grant's breath caught.

He smiled as her movement to hang her coat over her arm showed him just a peek of her slender leg through the split on the side of her dress. She was a feast for his eyes. Never had he seen such a beautiful woman. She was definitely a gift he planned on taking for himself. He swallowed the rest of his drink in one quick gulp, put his glass down and left his friends without another word.

When Grant reached the doorway the woman was standing at the window of the coat check. She handed the person there her belongings, then took the ticket from her and put it in her purse.

"Thank you," she said pleasantly and Grant quickened his pace to catch her.

* * * *

"Hello."
April turned to the voice at her back. *Okay, who's this guy?*
"Hello."
The man extended his hand. "I'm Grant."
April looked at his hand, then back at him. *Be nice, April.*
"Hello, Grant. I'm April," she said and walked away.
"Wait," Grant said picking up pace beside her. "That's a beautiful name, April. Do you mind if I walk with you? Are you here with someone?"
"Yes, I guess you could say that. I'm looking for someone."
"A boyfriend, a husband…?"
April stopped walking and gave him a sharp look.

Grant laughed and held his hands up in surrender. "I'm sorry. You are absolutely right. That was digging way too much into your business. You just met me. I have no right crossing the line like that."

April gave him a quizzical look, and continued on her way.

"So, April, can I get a minute of your time? Maybe get you something to eat or a drink perhaps?"

She stopped again and her puzzlement deepened, then her eyes widened as comprehension set in.

"Grant, are you—Are you trying to pick me up?" she asked on a stunned laugh.

Grant's face reddened at the accusation, but he nodded. "Guilty. Guilty as charged. I just, well, I saw you at the door and I just—" he stammered, then took a slow breath. "You're the most beautiful woman I have ever seen. I had to come over and take a chance."

His confession took her by surprise, but she was still suspicious of it. Grant didn't look like a psycho killer, though she had no idea what they really looked like. April a raised brow and looked him over. Even with her four inch heels, she still had to raise her gaze to meet his. Slim, but not at all skinny. Handsome in a preppy, Abercrombie and Fitch kind of way with his soft blue eyes and sandy brown hair, but it was his boyish grin he flashed at her earlier that caught her eye. Grant rocked on his heels as she checked him out. She almost smiled at his nervousness. Her gaze rose to lock on his. The light of intelligence looked back at her and hopefulness, but something else called to her that she couldn't quite put her finger on. Grant cleared his throat bringing April from her detailed scrutiny of him.

"If you're not interested, I'll just—"

April held up her hand and chuckled. "Now, wait a minute, Grant. Don't give up so easily. I mean, you did come all the way over here, in a soft-stalker kind of way." Her tone was teasing as she gestured to his whole body. "The least I can do is hear you out, right?"

Grant smiled, and then let out a relieved sigh. "Yes, I'd like that. Would you like to get that drink?"

April nodded. "Sure. I guess I have time for a drink."

Grant offered his arm and guided her to the nearest bar stand.

"Yes, sir, would you like to try our new cocktail Cupid's Arrow?" the bartender asked. "It's our specialty drink for today."

Grant raised a brow. "Cupid's Arrow? That's a terrible name for a drink. Did you choose it?"

The bartender chuckled. "Yeah, but it's better than the first name I came up with."

"Oh yeah? What was that?"

"Love Potion Number Ten."

Grant and April laughed.

"Yeah, you're right. Cupid's Arrow still sucks, but it's better than that," Grant agreed.

"It's smooth, sweet and has a nice kick. It's made for lovers. My concoctions have brought strangers together and existing couples closer," he explained with a wink. "Trust me. You're going to like it."

Grant and April laughed again.

"Okay, look, let me whip you up a sample cup. If you don't like it, I have lots of other stuff you could try too," the bartender urged.

Grant turned a disbelieving look to her. "Well, do you want to take a stab at it?"

April shrugged. "Sure. Let's do it."

"All right, I guess we'll be trying your special concoction, Mr. Bartender. Pour us up a couple of glasses."

"Excellent!"

He handed April and Grant a small paper cup of the bright pink liquid. April stared at it unsure. Grant looked into his cup with a questioning look on his face, too.

Uh-uh, girl. This was your idea. Suck it up and go for it!

April accepted her inner encouragement, holding her cup out toward Grant.

"You ready?" she asked with her best smile in place.

Grant smiled back. "Yup, let's do it."

She tapped her drink to his and they swallowed the contents at the same time. To her surprise the thick liquid was exactly as the bartender described it and she liked it.

"That's not bad," Grant said.

She giggled. "I was thinking the same thing."

"All right, bartender—"

"Joe," he supplied.

"All right, Joe," Grant amended. "It's unanimous. We like it. Give us a real one."

"Coming right up!"

April and Grant stayed at the bar not only indulging in more Cupid's Arrows, but several other drinks Joe recommended to them. They spoke on everything from current events to their favorite foods to how much she hated the weather. She was having a good time.

"I think I need to sit down, Grant. I have to back off the drinks and find some food. I didn't really have time to eat any dinner tonight."

"I know what you mean. I didn't either. Let's get a table."

There were people standing all around socializing. He took her hand and pulled her through the crowd as the people moved closer together, dancing to the beat of the music. The music was loud and eclectic, but she still heard him when he turned to speak to her.

They maneuvered through the dancers coming out the other side. April spotted an empty table and pointed. Grant shifted direction to head for it.

"So, tell me April, what brings you to this party?" Grant asked motioning for her to sit. "You're not really here with a husband or boyfriend, are you?"

She chuckled. "No, I'm not, but I am here with a boss. I'm supposed to be working. Well kind of."

"What do you mean?"

"I work for Spit Shine Cleaning Services. My boss is here to acquire new clients like everyone else I guess. He has a meeting set up to speak to someone tonight about using our services."

"I'm here with some colleagues who are hoping for the same. They invited me to come with them at the last minute. We're staying here at the hotel, but I really came for the party."

April giggled.

"So you're supposed to be with your boss when he has his meeting?"

"Yes, he prefers if it in case they ask something he doesn't know."

Grant laughed. "So you're brains of his operation? I like that. Why don't you tell me about it. What do you guys do?"

"Well, we do industrial cleaning. You know, like for big companies and stuff. We use our own supplies. When my boss comes to things like this it's really to push our product since you can hire anyone to clean."

"Does your stuff work?"

"Yes, it does. Shines better, cleans better, better for the environment, disinfects—"

Grant twisted his lips and April laughed. His pink bow lips looked so cute in that strange shape that she couldn't help herself.

"You're just saying that because you work there."

"No, it really does work. I have tried it on several different things around my own house and at the office and it works great."

He smiled. "Your boss should use you as a spokesperson or in commercials. I think clients want to hear from real people who actually use the product, not the hired actors who are paid to say it works."

"Customer knowledge does help with sales. I have been telling him that."

"Have you? You are way too intelligent to be his assistant."

"I won't always be his assistant."

"Ahh, beauty, brains and ambition. I like that in a woman."

April smiled at the compliment. "Thank you, Grant. You're very sweet. So tell me, if you tagged along with your friends, where are they?"

He shrugged and scooted closer to her. "I have no idea. I ditched them the moment I saw you."

April's eyes widened. "Really?" She watched him nod and was stunned that he would do so. She cleared her throat and fumbled with her fingers to distract against the heat on her cheeks in case he sensed her embarrassment. "Oh. So what do you do for a living, Grant?"

"I'm a chef. Perhaps you'll let me cook for you. I'm thinking a nice quiet dinner, and then breakfast the next morning," he added with a sly grin.

April saw the look of interest in his eye. Something she hadn't seen in a long time. She swallowed to wet her suddenly dry mouth.

He smiled at her, then stood.

"Let me see if I can find us something to eat around here. I'll be right back."

Grant left her at the table and April walked the edge of dancing people bouncing on her toes trying to see over their heads as she searched the crowd frantically.

"What are doing, April? Mr. Bowman is going to kill you if you don't find him soon. You are here to work, not to flirt," she chastised, then stopped walking. "Okay that must be it. I must have gone crazy," she muttered shaking her head.

Catching the glimpses of profiles here and there of people she didn't recognize only left her frustrated. She returned to the table just as Grant appeared with two plates of fruit, cheese, crackers and assorted meats. April looked at the plates, then back to him and he laughed.

"Hey, this is all I could get on such short notice. I didn't see any *real* food."

"It's fine. Look, Grant, I have to go. I'm having a really nice time with you, but I have to find my boss. I'm supposed to be working, remember? If I don't find him in this crowd soon, I'll be looking for a new job come Monday."

"Wait, no, please, April. Dance with me."

He took her hand tugging her gently to the dance floor.

"Dance? No, Grant, I shouldn't. I—"

"Come on, you know you want to," he teased. "Just give me one dance and I promise I'll help you find your boss. Okay?"

"Grant, for real, I really should—"

Grant pulled her into his arms, their bodies touching for a brief moment. The soft scent of his cologne reached her nose, a spicy, manly scent. He brought her hands to his mouth. Brushing his lips over her knuckles, he made his plea.

"Come on, please. One dance."

The close contact of his body and the gentle kiss he put on her fingers melted her protests.

"Well, okay...just one."

Grant's smile widened as he pulled her to the dance floor. A slow song played. They moved carefully with an invisible wall between them as she held on to his shoulders stiffly, attempting a waltz-like persona. The music changed smoothly into another song with a slower more sensual tempo. Grant dropped his hands to leave the dance floor, but April gave no sign she was done. She liked the current song better and relaxed into her stance. Grant quickly corrected himself and continued dancing.

When the next instrumental started April moved more fluidly to the music. Her arms slowly closed around his neck. Grant's grasp closed around her waist. Her body seemed to gravitate on its own toward him without her permission He held her tighter. April felt the firmness of his chest against her. She smiled to herself wondering what he would look like naked. With her face pressed against his shoulder, the faint beating of his heart relaxed her even more. His arms were strong and comfortable as they danced. His closeness felt warm and inviting and she realized she wanted him too. Grant's head dipped as he sniffed her shoulder loudly.

"God, you smell good. What are you wearing? I'm going to take stock in it first thing Monday morning."

She giggled. "It's Seductive Serenade."

"Yes, it's definitely that, but what's the name of it?"

The softness of his warm breath was sultry on her neck. "That is the name. You know, you're very charming."

"Am I? I'm not trying to be. I'm very serious."

April smiled. "I think I might have had a little too much of that Cupid's Arrow. I'm not feeling like myself right about now."

His hug was tighter for a moment as he spoke. "Neither am I, April, but I don't think it has anything to do with *that* Cupid's Arrow as much as the other Cupid's arrow."

April blinked a few times comprehending his words. She stopped dancing and stepped back to look at him. There was no teasing in the gaze he leveled on her. The gleam that shined back at her was lust filled. Grant wanted her. She had thought he was being playfully flirtatious, but the look of intent in his gaze told the true story. The obvious flames of desire burned as clear as day those eyes, that reminded her of a clear summer sky.

Grant's mouth opened and closed as if he wanted to say something but thought against it. His lips were perfectly shaped and soft looking. The kind of lips that would singe your skin with each kiss, melt away your inhibitions and leave a woman with a burning longing for more,. April had never been kissed like that, but had always longed for it. Her body responded to the sight, her nipples tightening in her bra, her inner walls pulsed making her panties damp. Without another thought, she leaned on her toes and caught them with her own.

Grant let out an accepting moan and returned her kiss. It was insistent and dominant. Tasting him sent tremors up and down her spine. He gripped her waist bringing her even closer to him. As the kiss deepened, her inner core was enflamed, throbbing frantically with the need to have him inside her. People continued dancing around them undisturbed by their actions as if it were normal for a couple to be kissing in the middle of the dance floor.

April felt his want for her too, hard and strong between them pressing against her pelvis. She ground against it instinctively wanting more of it. She sensed something different about Grant. Something she saw the moment he shook her hand and looked in her eyes. He was irresistible. The sensations he created within her were impossible to ignore. They soared through her system wreaking havoc on her mind and body. April was stunned at her body's reaction to the man. The scent of her desire for him reached her nose and she knew he could smell her also.

April pushed him back abruptly ending the kiss, breathing like she had run a mile. She stared into his eyes and he, too, was wide eyed and breathing hard.

"April, I'm sorry. My fault. I shouldn't have—"
She touched his lips. "Take me to your room, Grant."

Chapter Three

They left the dance floor and were on the nineteenth floor inside his room moments later. Grant lifted April from her feet and carried her to the bed.

"April, are you sure?" Concern filled his query. "I don't want you to feel—"

April touched his lips again and smiled. "Shh, you're breaking the mood. I'm fine."

His gaze searched her soft brown eyes. They sparkled with growing lust. The sight excited him more. Grant leaned forward and her eyes closed when his lips met hers again. The heat from their first kiss rocked his senses burning him from the inside out. Even in his haze of want and need for her he was conscience not to move too fast. She was the one. He knew it and didn't want to scare her away.

Reluctantly he released her mouth, then reached to her side to unzip her dress. She gasped.

"How did you know the zipper was on the side, Grant?" April asked in a shocked tone.

He chuckled. "I had a feeling that it was there even though I couldn't see it."

"You sound like you've had lots of practice undressing women," she teased.

"As a matter of fact, I have," he confessed with a laughing grin. "I'm the only boy of four, my sisters are all older. Believe me, I've had my share of locating and unzipping strategically placed zippers."

April laughed as she lifted her hips to help him. The sound was light and playful. He smiled when he heard it.

"House full of sisters huh? Well that's good to know."

"Oh yeah? Why?" Slowly he slid the dress from her body.

"Men who are raised by women have a better appreciation for the women in their lives."

"Mm, hmm, I would have to agree."

April lay on the bed in just a strapless black satin bra, black panties and black thigh high stockings. Grant took a slow breath as he feasted on her beauty. Her skin was flawless, her breast filled the bra seductively and her hips were rounded and soft. She was exquisite. He slid his hands over her legs, then suddenly chuckled.

"What?"

"Christmas wasn't that long ago, you know." He leaned forward to leave kisses over her exposed skin.

"Yeah?"

"I was just wondering what a man has to do to have *these* stockings hanging by his chimney with care *next* Christmas?" he asked bouncing his eyebrows with a mischievous grin.

April laughed. "Well you're definitely starting out right, that's for sure. Come here," she said and pulled him onto her.

Together they laughed and rolled across the big king-sized bed until she was on top of him. She rose and straddled his body sitting across his waist.

"Now, I get to do you."

"Oh, yes. *Please* do me," he said smiling wide.

She chuckled, then dropped a kiss on his lips. "You are too cute."

April undid the buttons on his shirt. She was beautiful even from his new position. He knew he could look at her for the rest of his life. She loosened his tie and pulled it away next. After opening his shirt, she ran her small hands through the hair on his chest and down his stomach. Goose bumps rose on his skin from her delicate handling.

"You have a very nice body, Grant. Tight chest, tighter abs and I love this hair," she said gliding her fingers over each area mentioned. "You're a very sexy man."

Grant's cock throbbed at her words. He swallowed to wet his suddenly dry mouth.

"Thank you."

April smiled moving back to purposely rub her bottom against the hardness beneath his pants.

"I think it's time to release the beast, don't you?"

Grant hoped the question was rhetorical because he couldn't find his voice to answer her at the moment. April lifted herself over his straining erection to sit across his legs. She opened his zipper and gave his pants a gentle yank, his hard-on sprang forth showing its vitality and eagerness.

Together they stood removing the last of the other's clothing and soon were before one another bare as the day they were born. Grant looked her over and his cock bobbed before him. The air was charged around them, the sparks of their attraction almost visible. He waited for her to make the first move, afraid he would pounce on her in his need to have her.

Luckily he didn't have to wait long. April reached around his neck and leaped onto him, making him catch her in his embrace. He guided her to the bed and pulled her on top of him, taking her mouth in a hungry kiss. That she engaged him just as lustfully excited him. April lifted her hips and he knew what she wanted. He adjusted his rod to an upright position and she buried his erection into her soft core. She broke the kiss with a gasp rising to sit up, sheathing him deeper within her body.

"Oh God, Grant," she breathed.

He gripped her hips and felt a shiver run across her skin. Goose bumps rose beneath his fingers and her nipples tightened before his eyes. The lust filled look on her lovely features accompanied by her body's reaction to him threatened to take him over the top instantly. April licked her lips and her head fell back as she rotated her hips, adjusting to him. Another shattered moan escaped her. With a slow breath, she fell forward to grip his shoulders. Her eyes were still closed and her full lips were parted. The sight entranced Grant.

She moved slowly at first, but as the slickness of her tunnel increased so did her movement. April groaned aloud at each downward thrust. The sound sent shudders up Grant's spine. He slid his hands over her soft brown skin, trailing them down her back, across her full hips and up her front to caress each breast. She was velvety smooth, extremely sensual and so very sexy.

April found her rhythm bouncing her ass over his staff and something caught fire within him. Her slender fingers tweaked his nipples increasing his pleasure ten-fold. His head spun like he was caught in a cyclone. A tidal wave of ecstasy lifted him higher increasing his journey to bliss.

Grant had never felt the way this woman made him feel! April was incredible! The feel of her, the way her body moved over him, the sounds she made, her scent! He held on to her hips sliding her back and forth then up and down encouraging her more. Her efforts caused him to scream unashamed and loud.

April's blazing tunnel teased the head of his lance over and over just before she swallowed him whole. It was glorious. He wanted to have as much of his staff inside her as he could get. Ecstasy built within at volcanic proportions. He couldn't stand it another moment. One of his heads would explode soon if he didn't regain some control quickly. With an animalistic sound he hardly recognized as his own, Grant reached around her waist and flipped her over. A startled yelp came from her, but she didn't seem displeased.

The strength and passion behind his actions surprised Grant as well, but it had to be done. Looking up into April's sensual face, as the scent of their love making hung in the air and her lovely breasts bobbed tantalizingly before his eyes, the sight would've taken him over the edge much sooner than he was ready. That wasn't how he wanted their encounter to end. Already he prayed they would be together like this again, for a lifetime if she left the decision to him. He would have to pleasure her beyond measure if the option was to become a reality. That was his main focus.

Grant stroked her heated walls with firm deliberate movements, digging deeper each time, slowing down the pace. A shiver of delight danced down his spine leaving goose bumps in its wake. It was magnificent. With every back and forth motion, Grant knew he had to have this woman, to make her his own. From the comfortable way they were with each other, the playful banter that came naturally to the passionate sounds and insistent thrusts beneath him, it all pushed him closer to Heaven's gates. April was special. Hearing her whimpers of pleasure knowing he caused them drove him to frenzy.

"April...Oh my God!"

He drove faster giving in to the raging bliss building inside him, unable to stop or slow it. Grant bit his lip as he delved into her again and again. He couldn't get enough of her! His head fell forward to look into her exquisite lust-filled face.

"Open your eyes, sweetheart. I want to see you when you come," he demanded breathlessly.

Her eyes sprang open filled with the fire of her desire. An uncontrolled inferno burned brightly inside them. Grant was consumed by the amber flames, drawn to the blazing light he saw. It called to his soul. He opened himself to what he saw and a portal into her being was offered to him.

Grant continued to pierce her with his erection in frantic abandon until they fell over the edge together screaming in combined rapture. His body exploded in a blaze of internal combustion. The sensation shook him almost violently as his seed was pulled from him. Exhausted, Grant collapsed on top of her and they both lay quietly gasping for air. When his heart rate finally began to slow, Grant rolled off her. He gathered April into his arms and held her fiercely close, drowning in the afterglow that was new to him.

* * * *

April lay in Grant's arms with a feeling of complete contentment. It was a new sensation. His body molded behind her, fitting perfectly. The hair on his chest was velvety soft against her back. His arm rested over her waist as he held her almost lovingly. She wiggled her fingers noticing they were laced with his and swallowed a sigh.

How could it feel so right with a man I just met?

But it did. His touch, his smell, the feel of him against her, in her and on her was all fairytale-like perfection. April wished they could stay as they were, but she knew they couldn't. The real world was right outside the door and it demanded their presence whether she wanted to go or not.

"Grant—" she started softly.

"I know," he replied interrupting her. "We have to go."

She nodded. "Yeah."

"Something strange just happened to me, April. Something wonderfully strange, that I have never felt before. I—I just don't want it to end so soon." He nuzzled her shoulder. "Does it have to?"

Grant hugged her close, his arms circling her protectively. April melted into his embrace and sighed.

I don't want it to end either, but yes, it does have to end.

The experience with Grant was amazing to be sure, but April refused to slip into denial on what it *really* was—a one-night stand with a hot guy at a hotel party. She simply let herself get carried away by Grant's extreme sexiness and willingness to give her an orgasm that wasn't self induced.

"April, I love you."

She gasped softly and stiffened at his announcement.

"I know that probably sounds like a line to you, but I do."

April turned over to face him, but she didn't reply. Grant pulled her closer.

"Do you believe in love at first sight? I do and I love you," he continued without waiting for an answer. "I knew it the moment I laid eyes on you. You're special."

April pressed her lips together. This was not what she expected. One-night stands don't end with declarations of love. She turned away from his burning stare, but he gripped her chin with his thumb and forefinger returning her gaze to him.

"I'm not crazy. I know what I feel. I don't want this to end."

His last words had finality in them, but April knew better. Good sex will make a man say anything for another round of the same. She caressed his face and let a knowing smile spread across her lips.

"Let's just see how we feel when we're not holding each other naked in the afterglow of wonderful sex, okay?"

Grant gave her a small smile, removed her hand from his cheek and kissed her palm. "I'm still going to feel the same way, April. This is not great sex talking for me. I've had that before. What I'm feeling is unique."

"Let's just see anyway."

He nodded with a defeated sigh, then let her go. April sat up on the edge of the bed for a moment. She felt cold and lonely outside of his arms and was reluctant to leave him.

"I'm going to take a shower." She looked over her shoulder at him. "You want to wash my back?"

His elated smile warmed her heart. Grant took her outreached hand and together they walked to the bathroom. In the shower, she watched the water run over Grant's muscular body. The hair on his head and his chest laid slick from its weight. April lathered her hands and slowly washed his chest playing in the whorls. She moved down to the rippling muscles of his stomach, wiping, playing, cleansing. Reapplying more soap, April moved to his sleeping member carefully stroking it back to life, from the base to the impressive ruby head she had seen earlier. It grew in her skilled hands and soon was back to its former glory.

Grant stepped out of her reach for a second, back under the water to rinse off and returned to her, pressing her against the shower wall. All thoughts of leaving him to return to the party left her mind as his growing erection teased the junction between her legs with the promise of bringing her more pleasure.

April held onto the shower pole. In the back of her mind she prayed that between the rough little fish on the bottom of the tub and the pole itself, they wouldn't fall and break their necks.

Grant held her against the wall. His hands and lips were all over her body. If it hadn't been for the water spraying at her from a distance cooling her heated skin April was sure she would have burst into flames. Just his kisses and touch alone sparked several mini orgasms within her. He was on his way to bringing her to another very large one, but he slowed to a stop.

His muscular arms lifted her with ease. Grant positioned her to the right spot easily holding her in place and sliding her onto his jutting erection. She didn't have to do a thing but hold on for the ride. And what a ride! He filled her completely. She felt every inch of him sliding in and out of her as he moved her up and down. Her sensitive nipples brushed teasingly against the hair on his chest. It wasn't long before the two acts together set off an explosion inside of her that left her body spent and her mind reeling.

Grant felt as hard as ever inside her when the spasms stopped. She knew he could easily have her on that wall coming again and again before he was done with her, but he had mercy on her. She gripped the bar breathing hard barely able to hold on as he pumped into her, coming shortly after she did. After a while April released the pole, Grant held her against his body until she caught her breath. When she eased her feet to the tub again, Grant backed up pulling his spent member from her. Grant stepped under the water and washed quickly. She reached around him to get a cloth to do the same, but he stopped her.

"Please, let me."

His hand slipped under the warm running stream to soap the cloth, then Grant softly washed his essence from April's body. She enjoyed watching his eyes widened as the water rushed over her breast when she rinsed off. Together they left the bathroom and hugged one last time. The reality that their time together was finally up seemed to hit them both at the same time. April saw the sadness in his lovely blue eyes when she kissed him once more. They took a moment to dry each other off, then redressed to return to the party.

Chapter Four

April stopped by the bar and ordered another Cupid's Arrow. Swallowing the first one quickly, she motioned for Joe to bring her another.

"Hey, where's your friend," he said refilling her glass.

"Oh, well, it's time for us to work so he went to find his people."

Joe nodded and moved on to service others. April scoffed and gulped down half the contents in the glass.

"You're the one who should be finding your people, April," she muttered to herself. "Yeah, it was the best sex you've had in over a year…well, it was the *only* sex you've had in a year, but that's not the point. Who am I kidding? That was the best sex I *ever* had. But was it worth losing your job over? That's the twenty-thousand dollar question."

The query settled into her buzzed brain. Her body still tingled from Grant's touch. She could feel the stretch in her thigh muscles and her pussy from riding him and a smile touched her lips as she raised her cup to finish her drink. When her drink was gone, April dropped the empty cup with a dull clunk, then groaned.

"I'm so fired," she said hanging her head.

"April, there you are."

She snapped her head upright and spun on her stool.

"I wondered if you were here yet. I'm so sorry I was late. The wife held me up asking a bunch of crazy questions. I told her I had to be here by eight o'clock since I told you to be here. As you can see that didn't matter to Mrs. Bowman. Here it is after ten o'clock and I've just been here about ten minutes," her boss said on a laugh. "I guess this doesn't count as fashionably late, does it? This is just plain ole late!" he added laughing harder.

Stunned by her boss' explanation, April could barely form a reply.

"Uhh…"

"Well, the good news is I've already found the client. Ran right into him as I was coming in the door. He is completely on board *and* he introduced me to a friend of his. The friend owns his own restaurant in Carmel and he's interested in our services as well!" he announced jovially. "So we've killed two birds with one party," he joked, then offered his hand to her. "Come along, April. I want you to meet them so we can seal the deal."

"Yes, sir."

"Since I hadn't found you yet I gave them a sorry proposal, but I explained that you were much better at that type of thing than I."

Full comprehension still wasn't restored. "Uh-huh."

He chuckled. "Are you all right?"

Finally her brain was back on track. "Yes, sir, I'm fine. Did you say you've only been here for a little bit?"

"Yes, not even a half hour. Sorry you were stuck here waiting on me. I know you really didn't want to come out to this shindig."

Relief flooded through her as he pulled through the crowd to a table. April couldn't help but smile at her good fortune. She could cherish the memory of her wonderful fling with Grant without it having a bitter end of losing her job behind it. They arrived at the table with the clients and her smile was replaced by a stunned intake of breath.

"April Harding, this is Daniel Robbins and Grant Murphy our new clients. Mr. Murphy owns Chef Murphy's Bistro. He's the friend I mentioned," he added close to her ear.

She swallowed her shock quickly putting her best smile in place. "Hello, Mr. Robbins, it's nice to meet you. Mr. Murphy, wonderful to meet you as well."

Grant stood and smiled at her. "The pleasure is mine in meeting you, April. What a beautiful name."

She could hear the lust in his voice as he kissed her hand. Her pulse raced as her body remembered his touch.

"Since Robbins here has already heard our shtick I will take him with me. April, will you bring Mr. Murphy up to speed on our products and how we do things since he will be joining our team?"

"Of course, Mr. Bowman."

"Excellent! This is cause for celebration. We shall return with drinks so that we can toast our new relationship. We're all going to be great friends from here on out."

April watched her boss leave then turned to Grant. "What happened? How did you become our new client?"

"When I found Dan he mentioned Mr. Bowman from Spit Shine called to tell him he was running late but would be here any minute. That's when I realized he was meeting your boss and by extension you."

Grant brought both her hands to his mouth and kissed her knuckles. April stepped closer to him. Her core throbbed reacting to his closeness. The near two hours she had spent with him were the best she had in a long time. Did she really want to give up the chance that it *might* work with him?

"Grant, you didn't agree to be our client just so we could have another chance to hook up, did you?"

"Absolutely not. I agreed because you convinced me that the product was good. I consider it a fringe benefit that I'll see more of you if we're working together."

"What kind of fringe benefits were you hoping for?"

She gasped as Grant pulled her against his torso. "I don't believe in coincidences, April, but I believe that everything happens for a reason. I think this whole situation is fate. This party, your boss running late, us meeting, our time together, it was all part of a divine plan."

"What plan?" she asked breathlessly.

He smiled. "The plan to bring us together. You probably don't believe in fate since you don't believe in love at first sight, but that doesn't mean it doesn't exist." He leaned in and kissed her gently on the lips. "Cupid lined up his arrow and you and I was his target. We belong together," he told her with a happy grin. "I want to be with you, by whatever means necessary. I want you to give me a chance to prove to you that love at first sight is real because I do love you."

Before she could form some kind of response to his affirmation, her boss and Mr. Robbins returned. April stepped out of his arms widening the space between her and Grant, but he made sure to stay beside her. The men handed them each a glass. Mr. Bowman raised his in toast.

"The bartender said this was some kind of special lover's drink or something. From the looks of the people in this place I wouldn't be surprised if he slipped some kind of aphrodisiac in it," he added with a chuckle. "Anyway, to us and a long association together!"

Grant raised his glass with everyone else, but his eyes never left April's. "My sentiments exactly," he whispered to her.

They drank together and she moved closer to him. "I think Mr. Bowman may be right about the drinks. The bartender may have slipped us all a Mickey," she said shaking her cup.

He chuckled. "Everyone does look a little looser than they did earlier."

"So you're agreeing that *everyone* got slipped a Mickey?" April teased with a raised brow.

Grant laughed. He took her hand and pulled her to the side away from the other men.

"That doesn't go for us, baby. What we got growing between us has nothing to do with the drinks. That, sweetheart is plain old fashion love."

"Well, since you feel so strongly about it I was thinking the least I can do is let you convince me."

Grant slipped his hand around her waist and yanked her to him. She gasped as an exhilarating tremor ran through her body. His lips brushed across hers as he spoke.

"I think that would be a benefit to us both."

Her body heated for him again. Maybe he was right. She would be crazy to let go of a man that could arouse her so easily without even seeing if it would work.

"I—I wasn't a big fan of Valentine's Day before today," April confessed.

He smiled. "Well I'm going to have to change that. I'll start by making this the first of a series of '*best* Valentine's Day of all' for you."

THE END

Accidental Valentines
by
Daisy Dunn

Chapter One

    Alex stood in front of his high-rise office window overlooking the city of Chicago late in the evening. His firm was situated on the fifty-ninth floor, making streetlights and neon signs appear as tiny burst of dotted lights breaking through the darkness. On this bitter cold February night, a gentle snow fell blanketing the city, making the evening seem calm. The peace and tranquility he felt at the moment had been the most he'd experienced in months. Seeing his bitter wife Sally made him dread every second of returning home.

    They'd drifted apart in the past few years and fighting seemed to be their only means of communication. *Sally's changed or maybe I have.* Warring with his emotions, he decided to ask his wife to go for marriage counseling with him. At thirty-eight years old, he didn't want to throw away ten years together. Lately, he found himself working longer hours, so he wouldn't have to face the chaos and anger greeting him at the door almost every night. The time had come for him to stop ignoring the problems—whatever they may be—and find a solution for both their sakes.

    Taking a deep breath, he sighed, knowing he had to leave his cocoon of safety and solitude. Sorrow filled his heart as he turned away from the window, and headed out of his office, forcing himself to go home.

    Twenty minutes later, he parked his Mercedes in the garage. Composing himself for their talk tonight, he took a few minutes to go over the situation in his mind. *Please let her listen to me.*

    He emerged from his vehicle and entered the house through the side door. Hanging up his coat and taking off his shoes, he wasted as much time as possible before having to face Sally. Finally, he walked into the living room and noticed her suitcases sitting beside the front door. He turned and headed into the kitchen and found her leaning on the counter writing something on a pad of paper.

"Hi, Sally."

"Oh, you startled me. I didn't hear you come in. I've been writing you a note."

"Why are your suitcases by the front door?" His muscles tensed, and he prepared himself for the worst.

"I'm getting ready to leave," she answered with a smug smile.

"Where are you going?"

"Well, if you haven't figured it out, I guess I'll have to spell it out for you. I'm leaving you for another man. I've been having an affair for over a year, and he wants me to move in with him." Scowling, she strode over to him and started jabbing him in the chest with her long fingernail. "You're such a useless man. I want nothing more to do with you. I'll be talking to a lawyer next week, and as you know, half of everything is mine."

Alex stood before her dumbfounded. With his heart in tatters, and knowing things weren't the best between them, he had honestly wanted to make their marriage work. This hadn't been the first time she cheated on him. After the last incident she begged him to give her another chance. This time, there would be no second chances.

"Leave." He clenched his jaw to keep himself from saying anything else.

"Gladly. At least Kevin will be there for me instead of leaving me by myself all the time. And the sex sure as hell is better!" Glaring at him, she bated him for an argument as usual.

Instead, he walked to the front door, opened it, and stood back, giving her plenty of room to march out of their house. Grabbing her purse off the kitchen counter and two bottles of wine, she looked at her bags, and then back at him. "Aren't you going to put them in the car for me?"

Aghast of her audacity, he looked at her with pure disgust. "Get your own bags."

"Never mind, I'll send for my things in the morning. By the way, happy Valentine's Day, darling."

He had forgotten what day it had been, but for years the occasion had lost all romance for him, as had his marriage. Angry, he watched as she sauntered into the night and out of his life, this time for good. Slamming the door behind her, he went to his den to pour himself a scotch on the rocks.

With a fresh drink in his hand, he turned on the gas fireplace and sat in his favorite brown leather chair. Gazing into the fire, he nursed his drink for a while thinking about what had transpired tonight and found himself quite relieved, as if a giant weight had been lifted off his shoulders. He loathed her right now, but brought up his glass in a toast. "Here's to you, Sally, may you be someone else's problem for a change. Good riddance."

* * * *

Catrina sat on the couch reading a book as her cell phone rang, breaking the silence in the room. Reaching over to the coffee table, she hoped her husband would be the one on the other end of the line. The number displayed on the screen made her smile. *It's him.*

"Hello, Phil."

"Hello, doll. Sorry about the late night. We just got out of our meeting and both sides have agreed to the terms of the merger. Bring out the champagne because we're going to celebrate tonight."

"Oh, that's wonderful news. I'm so happy for you. All you're hard work has finally paid off."

"Yes, it has. I know we didn't make plans for Valentine's Day because of this merger, but since I'm the boss, I told everyone I'm taking a week off to spend with my beautiful wife. However, I didn't tell my employees I intend to spend that time ravishing the hell out of you and treating you much better than the neglected wife you've been."

"I'm so excited. I'll get the champagne out and ready for your arrival."

"Perfect. I'm getting into my car now, and I should be home within half an hour. Would you mind wearing that slinky, black negligee I love so much?"

"I'm already two steps ahead of you. I'm wearing it right now." Catrina giggled like a school girl waiting for her date to come home.

"I'll see you soon."

"Phil?"

"Yes?"

An uncertain feeling overcame her and she blurted out, "I love you."

"I love you too, sweetie. Bye for now."

"Bye."

Her heart beat a little faster as she stared at her cell phone after hanging up. Something troubled her, but she couldn't say what. Shaking her head, she placed the phone back on the coffee table. *Maybe I'm feeling anxious for him to come home.* She shrugged her shoulders and headed into the kitchen to get the champagne ready for their romantic Valentine's evening.

A loud knock echoed through the quiet house. Catrina jumped, feeling groggy and unaware of her surroundings at first. Sitting up, she realized she'd fallen asleep on the couch waiting for Phil to return home. *When is he going to learn to stop forgetting his key?*

She walked to the door anxious to strut her satin and lace barely-covered body in front of him. Something told her they wouldn't even make it to the champagne. The knock came again, but this time a voice erupted through the door. "Mrs. Catrina Lund? This is the police. Please open up."

She froze, confused. *What the hell would the police want with me? I'm a law abiding citizen.* Returning to the couch, she grabbed her pink robe lying on the armrest, put it on, and went back to the door. Looking through the peephole, she saw two large uniformed police officers standing on her front step, a dusting of snow accumulating on their dark hats and broad shoulders.

Opening the door a crack, she said, "Yes?"

"Are you Mrs. Catrina Lund?" the taller of the two men asked.

"Yes I am. What seems to be the problem?"

"Can we come in, ma'am?"

"Of course, come in. It's pretty cold out tonight." She opened the door wide enough for both men to come in.

All of a sudden, one of them had a call coming through from the radio attached to his shoulder. "I'm going to have to take this. I'll be right back," the shorter man said. Disappearing into the falling snow, he seemed to be engulfed by the flakes in a matter of seconds.

"I'm Officer King and that's my partner, Office Vicks." He made his introductions as he stepped inside and closed the entrance.

"Can I get you a cup of coffee?" Confused, she didn't know what the proper etiquette was for a night time visit from the cops. She realized they weren't here to arrest her, or they would have done it by now.

"No, thank you, Mrs. Lund," he said as he took his hat off. Standing before her, he appeared nervous or at least anxious about something.

"If you're looking for my husband, he should be home soon. I got off the phone with him I think about half an hour ago. I'm not positive because I feel asleep on the couch."

"At what time did you last speak with him?"

"Around eight o'clock. Why? Has he done something wrong?" Turning, she glanced at the clock in the hallway. "Two forty-five? I can't believe he didn't wake me up. I'll run up the stairs and get him for you."

"No, ma'am. That isn't necessary. This is about your husband."

"What? I don't understand?"

"I'm so sorry to tell you this, but your husband has been killed in a head-on car crash. We don't know all the details yet, but we were informed he died upon impact. He didn't suffer."

The words flew inside her and wrapped around her heart, bursting it into pieces. "No, you're mistaken. I'm positive he's upstairs. Please let me go get him, please, I beg you, let me get him." Tears welled in her eyes, as she fought to understand the obvious lies Officer King told her.

"No, Mrs. Lund. Your husband is not upstairs." Reaching into his heavy coat, he pulled out a manila envelope. "These are his belongings."

With sadness in his expression, he handed the package to her, but she took a step away from him shaking her head. "No, I can't take that, it doesn't belong to him. Whatever's in there, it's not Phil's. I'm telling you, he's not dead, he can't be. I just talked to him."

"Is there someone I can call for you, a family member or friend to come and be with you?"

"No."

"I'm going to leave this for you right here," he said as he set the envelope on the ground in front of her as well as a business care. "When you're ready, you can open it up. If you need to talk to someone, I've left you a card with a support line phone number on it. Please don't hesitate to call them at anytime. I'm so sorry for your loss." Placing his hat back on his head, he nodded to her, and hustled out of her house without looking back.

She stood in the hallway staring at the package for what seemed like hours. Numb. Hoping she would soon wake up from this nightmare. *Maybe if I look at the items the officer gave me, it will prove he's not dead.*

With a tiny glimmer of hope, she bent over and picked up the envelope. Standing up, a tremor crept into her hands as she ripped the seal off. Inside she found a set of keys, a wallet and a plain gold wedding band. *Stop it, Cat, lots of men have plain wedding rings.*

Reaching in, she pulled out the simple ring. She took a deep breath and looked to see if it had been engraved. Her hands shook worse than before, making it difficult to focus on the inside of the band. Noticing some writing, she held it closer to her eyes to make sure she read it correctly.

My love, my life, forever...Catrina

Phil had died, and now she had her proof. The envelope fell from her hand, spilling the contents on the floor. Catrina followed suit, collapsing in a heap. The overwhelming loss hit her as the denial was swept away and the truth came flooding into her soul knowing she would never see him, touch him, or love him ever again. Her heart shattered as the realization of his death opened up torrents of tears she didn't try to hold back. Lying on the floor, she held his ring tight in her hand, and wept until she fell asleep.

Chapter Two

Almost five years later, and one week before Valentine's Day...

Catrina woke up to an incessant beeping blaring in her bedroom. Reaching for her alarm clock, she hit the snooze button, but the noise didn't seem to stop. She sat up and looked around her darkened room. The sun hadn't risen yet, and when she focused her blurry vision on her clock, it read ten after six.

"What the hell is going on?" Throwing off the covers, she stepped out of her bed. A cold burst of air hit her nude body as she slid on her slippers and thin white terrycloth robe. Even in the dead of winter, she always slept naked, enjoying the freedom her body had to toss and turn unencumbered.

Her little white kitten, Dapple, lay at the foot of her bed watching her get dressed, his eyes appearing tired and weary. "Come on, baby. Let's see what's making all that noise."

The kitten stretched out, jumped off the bed and ran to her side. He lifted his paws to her leg, a sign he wanted to be carried. She scooped him up in to her arms and placed kissed on his forehead as she strolled out of her bedroom and into the hallway.

Annoyed, she walked to the front of her house, turning on the lights as she went. Looking out her bay window, she found the source of the noise. A moving truck seemed to be struggling to back up onto the neighbor's driveway. The truck beeped every time the driver put it in reverse and tried again to fight against the icy road and driveway. *Who the hell moves in the middle of winter?*

Sitting in the cushioned window seat, still cuddling her purring kitten to her bosom, she watched the movers finally make it up the slippery slope of the driveway. Irritation soon turned to laughter as the men turned out to be quite humorous to watch. After the entertainment died down and the beeping stopped, she waited while her precious elixir of caffeine brewed in the pot, then made herself a cup of coffee and toast, and fed Dapple.

After twenty minutes, she walked back to the window seat with her coffee and sat down. She hadn't met or seen her new neighbors, so her curiosity forced her to find out who they were. Her late husband had instilled in her the wisdom of getting to know her surroundings and the people in them because you never know when you might be in need of some help. Phil had always been so safety conscience when it came to her.

"Well, Dapple, why don't we go and visit the family next door later on tonight. Actually, I will. You get to stay in the warmth of the house."

Looking up at her with his sleepy, golden eyes and pink nose, he purred away as she picked him up and placed him on her lap.

* * * *

Catrina pulled her long, dark hair up into a casual, messy bun and applied a touch of makeup to enhance her light brown eyes and high cheekbones. Dressed in a casual pair of bootcut jeans and a red sweater, she checked out her look in her full-length mirror in her bedroom. *Why do I care so much about how I look tonight? I guess I want to make a great first impression.*

With a rush of excitement, she ran down to the kitchen and put together a welcome basket filled with a bottle of red wine, fancy cheeses and crackers, biscuits and a small box of imported chocolate. "Yummy, I could polish off this basket myself."

She set her present by the front door, put on her jacket and a pair of dress boots, then headed out to meet the new family. Walking onto their porch, she noticed the door sat ajar. She knocked, but no one answer. *I think I better let them know their door is open. This is a nice neighborhood, but thieves have been known to break in this area too.*

Pushing open the door all the way, she called out to anyone within earshot, "Hello? Is anyone home?"

No answer. Nervously, she stepped inside and shut the door behind her. *I guess I'll look around and see if I can find someone.* Removing her snow-covered boots, she wandered into the living room with her basket of goodies, dodging the boxes strewn about the room. "Hello?"

As she continued through the house, she heard some noise coming from her right. A door stood open, so she peeked inside. The large room had been unpacked already and filled with exercise equipment. Taking a step closer, her breath caught in her throat. A handsome man stood in the center of the room, his left side facing her. *He's so sexy.* A set of earphones linked to an iPod strapped to his muscular arm prevented him from hearing her. He didn't have a shirt on and from the sheen of perspiration covering his body, he'd been working out for a while.

From the angle she stood, it appeared he pumped a free weight in his hand. Stepping closer, and knowing she should leave, her legs seemed to betray her and inched closer to him. He had black hair, stood about six feet two inches tall, and his body looked in top physical shape. Mesmerized by his rippling muscles, she stared at him with lust. She hadn't felt a carnal appetite since Phil passed away. Her body woke up to feelings long forgotten, her core tingled with need.

Edging closer to his side, she soon realized he didn't have a weight in his hand. Instead, he held his impressive cock, stroking it. Shocked, she needed to turn and run away, but her gaze wouldn't leave his full hand.

Suddenly, he stopped. Tilting her head up, she realized with horror, she'd been caught watching him. Without panic, he tugged up the front of his track pants, and then pulled out his earphones. God, she wished an earthquake would hit the house and swallow her up, anything to break up this humiliating situation.

"I'm sorry, I didn't hear you come in," he said, not as sheepishly as she thought he should be.

Embarrassed, she remained speechless at first but then found her voice. "I'm sorry to interrupt. I, ah, well, this is for you."

Handing the basket she'd made to him, she lost her last vestige of armor protecting her from his gaze. *If I didn't know any better, I'd swear he thinks this is amusing.*

"Thank you so much. You're very thoughtful. I'm Alex, by the way."

"Nice to meet you, I'm Catrina. I live next door, and I wanted to welcome you to the neighborhood. Your door had been left open, so I came in to drop off this gift and meet the family," she rambled, not knowing what else to do. She looked into his hazel eyes, and felt her legs grow weak. He was too attractive for his own good.

"I don't have a family. I live all alone. I hope my being single explains what you've just witnessed."

Oh no, he didn't just talk about it! Mortified, she could feel her cheeks growing hotter by the minute and knew her face must be as red as her sweater. "Well, I'll see you around."

"I hope so, Cat."

With an awkward wave, she bolted out of the room before he could say anything else. She slid on her boots and ran out of his house to the safety of her own home. Once inside, she leaned her back against the door, her heart racing, and her thoughts filled with the vision of this man. "I hope I never see him again."

Later that night, Catrina lay in her bed looking up at the dark ceiling, her kitten curled up on her legs. Last time she checked the clock, it read one thirty-two in the morning, but she still couldn't sleep. She'd been disturbed by what she witnessed Alex doing, but even more uncomfortable with her reaction to him. *He stood there so calm after I caught him touching himself. He didn't seem embarrassed in the least. Well, why should he? I'm the one who barged into his home and watched him, when I should have walked away. Oh, why didn't I walk away?* Frustrated, she hit the palm of her hand against her forehead, scaring Dapple. Poor baby jumped straight up in the air, and took off running. Catrina knew he would wander the house for a little while chasing shadows and anything else he perceived as movement.

It didn't take long for thoughts of Alex to drift back into her mind. His strong back with a light sheen of perspiration flitted through her mind. Sensual thoughts ran through her head as she pictured herself walking up behind him and running her tongue up the middle of his back and nibbling on his ear. She couldn't deny he had awoken a sexual desire, which had lain dormant for so long. Her lips ached for his kiss and her pussy throbbed for his touch. Tossing the blankets aside, she looked down at her nude body. For the first time in almost five years, Catrina was in desperate need of release.

Fully aroused, she fondled her D-cup breasts with a gentle touch at first, stroking her sensitive skin and making her nipples tighten and double in length. She licked her fingers and brought them back down to her breasts, circling the tips of her nipples. The sensations were unexpected, but needed. Her juices flowed as a steady ache built between her legs. Moving her right hand lower, she ran her fingers up and down her wet slit, enjoying the feel of her own touch. *I wonder what Alex's touch would feel like.*

She dipped her finger inside the slick folds, skimming the hood of her swollen clit. The need for touch overwhelmed her. Applying a slow steady pressure on her nub, she rubbed her pussy back and forth, savoring every gentle caress.

She moved her other hand down to her snatch, plundering inside her core with two fingers. Her fantasy running wild, she imagined Alex working her pussy, thrusting in and out of her, and then lowering his mouth to capture her clit and inner lips. The image seemed to swamp her senses, pushing her closer to the edge. The exciting repertoire of sexual positions she pictured them performing had been all she could handle. Her muscles tensed, her back arched off the bed, her heart beat quicken, and she let her building orgasm wash over her as she screamed with unadulterated pleasure.

Her body collapsed against the bed, her breathing heavy. *Oh God, I needed that. I didn't realize how much until tonight.* Smiling to herself, a haze of sleepiness crested over her mind. She allowed herself to enjoy this brief pleasure Alex unknowingly gave her, for tomorrow, she would be wracked with guilt.

* * * *

The next morning, Alex woke up in bed in his new home. Looking around at his new bedroom, everything felt right. Even in the disheveled state the room lay in with boxes, clothes and furniture all over the place, this seemed like home. Ever since his wife walked out on him, he had been running on autopilot. Going to work, staying late and coming home were his daily routine and he knew the time had come for a change.

Selling his business and his house, he moved to a different area of the city, taking time to figure out what he wanted to do in life.

When Catrina walked in on him in the exercise room, she'd noticed he'd been embarrassed, but when he looked into the beauty's eyes, he'd forgotten their whole predicament. Without regret, he'd kept women at bay since his wife left, not wanting to get involved with anyone. However, he knew the life he'd been living hadn't been healthy. The realization hit him one day, and he knew he needed to change.

Lying in bed, his thoughts drifted to Catrina. She oozed sensuality but didn't seem to realize it. A faint smile lit up her face even though he could tell she fought with the horror of catching him in the middle of his lewd act. Her full lips alone were enough to tantalize him into sin. *I need to know more about her. I think I'll pay her a visit tonight, thanking her for the gift basket. It's the polite thing to do.*

Chapter Three

Curled up in a corner of her couch, Catrina surfed the web on her laptop, working on some research for her latest novel. She'd been a published author for years, but after Phil's death, she stopped writing, her creativity seemed to have dried up. However, two years ago, the urge to write had come back, the muse alive and well. She began penning a new novel and released it a year ago. Her fans eagerly bought up her new work, energizing her spirit to keep going.

With a heavy heart, she missed Phil, and always would. They were high school sweethearts and married not long after finishing college. She had never been with another man nor did she want to be until last night. The desire stirred up layers of guilt in her soul. In order to deal with the feelings of remorse, Catrina had decided over her morning coffee, she would keep her distance from Alex. This plan seemed the only logical solution to assuage the shame.

Dapple had been curled up beside her and suddenly perked his head up, his eyes alert, his ears turned toward the door. Dashing off the sofa, he ran to the front entrance as a loud knock echoed through her home.

Not expecting anyone, Catrina placed her laptop beside her and headed to the door. Spying through the peephole, she saw Alex standing on the other side. *Oh my God, what do I do?* Dapple broke her concentration by pawing at her leg. She picked him up and held him in her arms. *Oh, I'm being silly. Go see what he wants, then send him on his way.*

With false confidence, she opened the entryway and was greeted by the most handsome smile she had ever seen. He had deep dimples in both cheeks, adding to his boyish looks even though she noticed a slight touch of gray subtly mixed with the black hair along his temples.

"Hi, Cat."

"Hi, Alex. Can I help you?" Looking quite sexy, he stood before her in his black, pullover sweater, and jeans.

"I finished quite a bit of my unpacking and needed a break. I wanted to invite you over for coffee. I would love the company."

Catrina didn't know what to say. However, her body betrayed her, urging her to go back into his home, but her guarded heart seemed to be in control. "Well, I happen to be in the middle of work right now."

"Hey, who's this little buddle? She's so cute." Reaching out his hand to the kitten, he stroked his little tummy.

"His name's Dapple. He's only fifteen weeks old and already he's full of personality. A real charmer, some might say," Catrina said as Dapple wrapped his tiny paws around Alex's large hand and started licking his fingers.

"I have to admit, he's adorable. Can I hold him?"

"Sure, be my guest." Before she could pass him over, Alex slid his hands around the kitty, stroking her nipple with his fingertips.

An electrical shock jolted through her body filling her full of desire. Holding the little kitten close, he nuzzled Dapple's forehead. The kitten seemed to thrive on the attention as he rubbed his furry face all over Alex. Catrina found herself staring at two of the most unlikely friends. Alex didn't seem to mind showing affection to animals and his kindness impressed her.

Turning back to her, he held Dapple against his wide chest and said, "The offer for coffee still stands. It's already brewed and waiting for you."

"All right, you twisted my arm. Let me feed the little beast, and then I'll be right over."

"I'll be waiting for you," he said beaming at her, his full lips smiling seductively.

Twenty minutes later, Alex welcomed Catrina into his home and ushered her into the living room. Looking around, she couldn't believe the difference a day of unpacking made. His black leather, sectional sofa, a gorgeous area rug and a coffee table took up the space instead of the boxes she had to step between yesterday. A fire roared in the corner casting a flickering glow into the room. The lights weren't off, but Alex had dimmed them.

"You've done a great deal of work in here today. It makes you want to snuggle together on the couch," Catrina said to her horror. "I mean, snuggle up with a good book and a blanket." She tried to cover up her blunder.

"I think I know what you meant," he said as he winked at her. "What do you take in your coffee?"

"I like it black."

"Well, I guess we like it the same way. We now have something in common." Alex disappeared into the kitchen and came back a minute later with two full coffee mugs, handing one to Catrina.

"Thank you."

"My pleasure, Cat. Please, have a seat on the couch, and I'll try to refrain from snuggling you. However, I make no promises."

A shiver ran through her body as she wondered what it would feel like to be held tight in his strong arms. The idea hadn't been an unpleasant one in the least. She sat down on the sofa, a little vexed, and watched as he sat closely beside her, his thigh touching hers. The heat from his leg seared through the fabric of her jeans, and she felt the rush of excitement filling her core.

Edging away from him a few scant inches, she hoped he would get the hint, but instead, he leaned toward her and gave her a devilish smile.

"I had reasons other than coffee for asking you here tonight."

Nervously, she sipped from her mug and asked, "What other reason?"

"Well, I wanted to say I'm sorry for what you witnessed yesterday."

"No, please don't. You have nothing to apologize for. I walked into your home unannounced. It's completely my fault." She hoped to never talk about that incident ever again.

"I didn't handle the situation very well, and the more I thought about it today, the more I realized how uncomfortable I made you, pretty much like I'm doing now."

"Thank you for your thoughtfulness. I appreciate your candor."

"Can I be honest with you about something else?"

Catrina's stomach flitted with butterfly wings, while a slow blush warmed her cheeks. "Sure." She sounded more confident than she felt in his close proximity.

"I find you an engagingly beautiful woman. I haven't been in a relationship in years, and I haven't wanted to get close to anyone.

However, you not only caught my attention, yesterday, but held it. I couldn't stop thinking about you all day. I want to get to know you more and see where this could lead."

"You're straight to the point, aren't you?"

"I don't believe in dancing around the subject. In my past, I've made the mistake of not speaking my mind, hiding my head under a rock, if you will, and I've promised myself I won't ever hide from the truth again. Cat, you seem to have enchanted me, for lack of a better word, and I can't get you out of my mind, nor do I want to."

"I don't know what to say."

"Are you single?"

"Yes."

"Do you find me attractive?"

Admiring his honesty and directness, she felt he deserved the same respect. "Yes, I do."

Alex reached out and took the mug away from her hands, placing it on the coffee table in front of them. Sitting back on the couch, he leaned toward Catrina. With a gentle touch, he ran his fingers up her arm to her face, and caressed her cheek. Without hesitation, she tilted her head into his palm, relishing the intimate touch so long ago forgotten.

His head came down, and his lips brushed with the lightest touch against hers. No other man had ever kissed her beside Phil, and Alex stirred up a fire burning deep inside. Terrified, she wanted to run to the safety of her home, freeing herself from any entanglement and complication she knew he would bring into her simple life, but her body longed for his sensual embrace, his deep kisses and wild abandon. Desire coursed through her causing her pussy to throb with need. The chemistry between them could not be denied, nor could their passion.

Catrina lifted her arms around his neck and pulled him to her, their lips crushing together. Sweeping his tongue inside her mouth, she flicked him back with her own. Tenderly, he pushed her down onto the couch and crawled between her legs, grinding his swollen rod against her core through their jeans.

Arching her hips, she urged him to press into her harder. Obliging eagerly, he moaned, and then he pulled away from her to remove his sweater. In a growing state of arousal, she took him in with her gaze. His body looked magnificent. He worked out, and it showed. She wanted to trace every ripple and line in his muscular chest, arms and abs. However, he had something else in mind. Reaching down, he removed her sweater with ease and unclasped the hooks on her hot pink push-up bra.

He moved the bra cups aside, exposing her breasts to his hungry gaze. Her dark, pink nipples hardened under the heat of his stare. "Oh my God, you are so damn sexy." Lowering his head to her chest, he started feasting on her breasts. He ran his tongue up and down the length of her swollen tips, and then took one into his mouth, while he cupped her other breast and rolled her nipple between his fingers.

"Your touch feels so good," Catrina said with her head rolled back and her eyes closed. She fisted her hands in his thick hair, urging him to continue his sensual touch.

Eventually, he moved down her body, placing wet kisses on her stomach to the top of her jeans. Undoing her pants, he backed off enough to remove them from her body. Alex looked down at her, taking in her hot-pink thong, which matched her bra. "Oh, Cat, I have to taste you," he demanded, positioning himself between her legs, so his face lined up with her pussy.

Catrina didn't realize what he'd meant until he pulled the edge of her thong to the side and placed his full lips on her swollen clit. Shocked by his actions, she tried to pull away at first, never having experienced this kind of intimate kiss from a man, but he held her with a firm grip. He worked magic with his tongue, sliding it back and forth with the right amount of pressure. Between the hypnotic rhythms of his steady licks and the pure bliss manifesting in her snatch, Catrina released her fears and hesitations of this sexual embrace. Relaxing back against the couch, she found her hips lifting of the own volition against his mouth. *I've never felt this sensual torture before. I wonder what else I've missed.*

Feeling her orgasm building, she yearned for relief. "Oh God, yes, yes!" Her body shuddered and came with an incredible force, wracking her to the core. Her pussy throbbed with uncontrollable contractions as she tried to catch her breath.

Alex pulled away from her and stood up beside the couch. Watching him as he removed his jeans and underwear, he stood naked before her like a Greek God. *He's so dam hot, I can hardly stand it!* She focused her gaze on his massive erection, with a drop of precum formed on the swollen head. His balls were tight, his pubic hair trimmed short, and the ridges of his cock promised long nights of pleasure.

Scooping up her petite form into his arms, he carried her into his bedroom, placed her ass on the edge of his bed, and bent over to grab her calves. Lifting her legs, he positioned her ankles on his shoulders. With a firm hold of his rod, he placed the head against her wet slit, running it up and down her slick folds combining their juices.

She couldn't move away, nor did she want to. As he loomed, looking large, masculine and powerful, the lock around her heart weakened. She wanted to open up to Alex, let him in. His cock slid into her opening and she wiggled her hips, encouraging him to go deeper. Moving her legs around his waist, he leaned over her body and said, "I could fall hard for a woman like you." He kissed her fiercely, possessing her lips as he thrust hard into her pussy, filling Catrina fuller than she's ever experienced. The hunger for his next thrust, uncontrollable with pleasure, swamped her senses.

Recklessly, he pulled out and slid back into the heat of her core.

"Faster," she whispered when he released her lips.

Obliging her command, he started to pound into her snatch faster, deeper, and harder. As she suspected, every ridge of his cock brought exquisite delight. Reaching the pinnacle of her desire, she fell into the abyss in a sensual euphoria. She tried to cry out, but he kissed her, robbing her of words and breath.

When he released her lips, he looked into her eyes. "Cat, you're so fucking desirable." His body tensed, and he thrust one last time before filling her full of his cum. A fine sheen of perspiration covered his body as she wrapped her arms around him.

Pulling out of her core, he collapsed beside her on the bed and wrapped his arm around her, drawing her tight against him. They lay together for a quiet spell, catching their breaths. Alex broke the silence after kissing her cheek tenderly. "You're amazing, my little Cat."

Catrina had never been called that before. She loved the endearment as it warmed her soul. "You weren't too bad yourself."

"I think it's important to tell you that I don't sleep around with women. In fact, it's been quite a long time since I've allowed myself to get close to anyone. I'm steadily growing attached to you already. I hope I'm not scaring you off."

"I'm very flattered you're feeling this way about me..."

"But?"

"But what?"

"I'm sensing 'it's been nice, but I only want to be friends' speech."

"Wow, did you sense the wrong thing." She giggled at him and continued, "I was going to say I haven't allowed anyone near me in years either, physically or emotionally. You're the first man I've desired or been with since my late husband passed away years ago, and I'm finding myself not only attracted to you on the outside, but also on the inside. I've let my guard down with you, something I haven't done with anyone."

"I'm so sorry to hear about your husband passing away. I guess that's something else we have in common. My wife passed away years ago too. I'm so honored and thrilled you've let me in. I can promise you one thing, Cat, I won't ever hurt you."

"You've made a pretty bold promise. There are no guarantees in life as we both know."

"You're right, but I don't want to go through my whole existence being cynical. I want to start enjoying my life with the woman I love standing beside me. I guess I've learned I'm a romantic at heart."

Alex's sweetness tugged at her heart. Clearly he wanted someone in his life, and he understood what it felt like to lose someone you love. *Maybe this might work out after all.*

"You sure seem romantic."

"I've learned from my mistakes in my marriage. I want to cherish the woman I'm with, not take her for granted. And I want the same in return."

"It sounds like we're kindred spirits."

"I'm starting to think so." Leaning over, he kissed her passionately.

Returning his kiss with the same ardor, the desire grew between them again.

Chapter Four

    The new lovers had been inseparable for three days. They'd spent time at each other's home having dinners, talking till all hours of the night, and making love where ever and whenever the frequent urge hit them.
    They curled up together on his couch in front of the roaring fire, enjoying a glass of red wine while soft music played in the back ground.
    "Alex, can I ask you about your wife?"
    "Of course you can. What do you want to know?"
    "I get the strong impression you and your wife didn't have a loving relationship. Am I right?"
    "Yes, you're right. The night she died, she left me for another man. I blamed her for the demise of our marriage and her countless affairs. But, after all this time, I realized we never loved each other right from the beginning. We went through the motions of married life, nothing more."
    "How long has it been since she passed away?"
    "It will be five years ago this Valentine's Day."
    Alex felt Catrina's body tense up in his arms, and he pulled back to look at her, noticing her face had gone pale.
    "How did she die?" she whispered, as he watched tears welling up in her eyes.
    "Are you all right, Cat?" Confused, he didn't understand why she'd be getting so emotional.
    "How did she die?" she asked again, demanding an answer.
    "The night she ran out on me, visibility was low due to a heavy snowfall. According to the police report, she thought she'd been driving in the correct lane, but it turned out she'd drifted into on-coming traffic. She drove head-on into another vehicle and died upon impact, or so I'm told."
    Horror crept into her face, as she stood up suddenly. "I have to go."
    "What is it? What's wrong?"
    "I have to go," she repeated almost running to the front door.

"Catrina, what's going on? Please, talk to me." Chasing after her, he grabbed her upper arms.

"Let go of me." Tears flowed down her cheeks.

"Not until you tell me what's wrong."

"I can't, I don't want to talk about it. Please, let me go home. I can't see you anymore."

"What? No, Cat, how can I let you go in the state you're in? Why don't you come back into the living room, sit down with me, and tell me why you can't see me anymore. I think I at least deserve your honesty." His heart broke watching her emotional melt down, and knowing he couldn't do anything to help her without her telling him the problem. The thought of losing her felt as if he had been punched in the gut.

Sobbing into her hands, she finally pulled back and looked at him, anger flashing in her eyes. "You're wife killed my husband."

He heard her words, but it took a while to register what she meant. Releasing her arms, his mind soared in several directions at once. She slipped on her boots and ran out of his house, while he stood staring after her retreating form.

He felt torn. One side of him screamed to run after her, get her to understand how he felt about her. The other side urged him to stay home and let her deal with the grief on her own.

"Dammit!" Marching into his living room, he stood there not knowing what to do with himself. "I fucking love this woman. What the hell am I doing here?"

Running back to the door, he bent over to put on his boots. Again, he stopped himself. He knew Catrina would always love her late husband, and the emotions she felt was her grief bubbling up to the surface. *I need to give her some space to sort things out, but a few days is all she's going to get. After that, I'm fighting for her with everything in me.*

Heading toward his homemade gym to work out, he hoped to clear his head from the confusion of the horrible coincidence they both discovered tonight.

* * * *

Catrina lay on her bed sobbing. *Why did it have to be his wife? Why?* The wall started to build around her heart again. *Every time I look at him I'll be reminded of Phil's death.*

Already fighting with the guilt of starting a new relationship, and recognizing the connection between them had been sullied, she couldn't continue seeing him. Regretfully, she'd let her guard down, allowing him into her life like no one else. However, she decided to end it now rather than later. Losing Alex hurt deeply, but she thought it would be better to end things before they went any further or used the 'L' word. Tonight she'd allow herself to wallow in self-pity and grief, but tomorrow she'd get to work on her novel, shutting out the world, especially Alex.

She wrote non-stop for days, purposely losing herself in the story, so she wouldn't have to deal with Valentine's Day or think about Alex in anyway. The sun had set, and still she sat at her kitchen table typing on her laptop. A knock at the door startled her, and she realized she was sitting in the dark, only the glow of her laptop screen illuminating the room. *Maybe they'll go away, whoever it is.*

Dapple ran to the door and mewed frantically at it, as if answering the person on the other side.

"Little traitor," Catrina said as she walked over to the entrance. Peeking through the peephole, she saw Alex standing on the other side. Her heart beat faster, and she put her hand on the wall to steady herself. He looked so handsome, yet distressed. Wanting to hold him tight and kiss the sadness away from his face, she struggled with the urge knowing she could never be that intimate with him again. Taking a deep breath, she opened the door.

"Hi, Alex."

"Hi, Catrina. Can I come in?"

"I don't think that's a good idea, do you?"

"Actually, I think it's a great idea. We need to talk."

Looking into his somber eyes, she knew she couldn't turn him away. *I'll hear what he has to say, and then I'll say a final goodbye.* "All right, come in."

He stepped inside and removed his winter coat and boots while she turned on the lights. Dapple seemed to sit patiently, waiting for Alex's hands to be free. Once he stood up, the kitten pawed at his leg to be picked up.

"I think Dapple missed me."

"I believe your right. You can have a seat and bring the little monkey with you."

Grabbing the kitty around the middle, he carried him into the living room, all four of his little paws dangling past Alex's hand. He sat on the couch and she felt his gaze burning into her soul. She sat on the love seat across from him, giving herself a buffer zone from his advances. Ready for this to be over with, she stared at the floor, trying desperately not to look at him.

"Catrina, thanks for talking to me. I know this isn't an easy time for you."

"No, Valentine's Day is a tough for me to get through. I can imagine it's not so hard for you to deal with."

"You're wrong there. I may not have been in love with my wife, and angry by what she did to me, but I didn't hate her, and I most certainly didn't wish her dead."

"But I loved my husband, and she took him away from me."

"Their deaths were an accident. I'm not defending Sally's behavior, but I know she didn't plan to kill anyone, let alone herself on that fateful night. She left me to go to her lover and live with him. Can you imagine the guilt I felt knowing she died while leaving me? If only I could have been a better husband, if only I could have loved her, and if only I spent more time with her, maybe she'd still be alive. Her death is a heavy burden I've had to carry around. I've learned to deal with it, but Valentine's Day reminds me about it all over again, and I can't help but feel remorse and sadness."

A wave of pain flowed into her heart and tears trickled down her cheeks. "I don't know what to do."

Alex lifted Dapple off his lap and set him down on the couch. Rising, he walked to Catrina and knelt down before her, taking her hands in his. "Let me help you through this. From what I've found out about you over the past week, you've gone through this alone. You had no family or close friends to turn to. Well, being alone ends now. I'm here for you, and I don't intend to go anywhere without you by my side."

"It doesn't seem right, I feel so guilty," she said as her body trembled with emotion.

"Dammit, Cat, I've fallen in love with you. You're a beautiful woman, both inside and out, and I want to spend every day of my life showing you how much I love you. Please, give us a chance. Don't let some horrible coincidence taint what we have. I believe their time had come to an end in this world, and maybe Fate meant for us to be together all along. Don't let guilt rule your life. Let your heart make some decisions for a change."

As his grip on her hands tightened, his words hit a nerve deep inside of her. She'd been living a sheltered life, hiding away from the world, relationships and people in general. Alex had been the first person she'd let her guard down with, and being with him felt right, from the initial embarrassing moment she met him. *He loves me. Maybe it's time to let someone in. Oh my God, I do love him.* Pulling her hands away from him, she wiped the tears from her eyes and faced Alex head on. "I've been afraid to fall in love again. Then I met you, and in such a short time, I've fallen in love with you too. This is all new to me, and I don't know if I'm going to handle things right or not. Could you handle being with a woman who loves another man?"

"I'm not here to replace Phil. I'm here to be a new love in your life at a new time in your life. I never want you to forget him, your marriage, or the love you two shared. Grieve for him, talk about him, love him, but know you're with me, and I'm here for you, to love you and cherish you until the day I die."

"I'm so afraid to love you, because I couldn't bear to go through another loss like I did."

"Cat, I don't mean to sound harsh, but dying is part of living. We're all going to leave this Earth at one point or another, but why not be happy and fulfilled while you're still alive. You need to live, sweetie. Phil would be heartbroken if he knew you weren't moving on with your life."

Alex spoke the truth, and she knew it. She couldn't deny herself the love he offered and the happiness he brought to her life. The time had come to move on. Promising herself she would never forget Phil, she knew he wouldn't want her to lock herself away, mourning his death for years to come. Placing her hands on Alex's face, she looked into his eyes. "I love you, Alex, and I want to make this work between us."

His smile lit up the room and his dimples made her weak. *How could I ever say no to this loving man?*

"You have made me the happiest man on Earth." Leaning forward, he kissed her lips tenderly.

Loving the feel and taste of him, she open her mouth eagerly to his invading tongue. The passion built between them, and Catrina could feel her pussy growing wetter with every kiss. Finally, she managed to pull away from his lips and asked, "Shall we go to the bedroom?"

Right away, he responded to her loving request. Standing, he picked her up in his arms and carried her to her bedroom with strong, determined strides. Once in her room, Alex set her down in front of her wardrobe. Undressing quickly, he stood before her naked, vulnerable, and sexy. He reached toward the hem of her sweater and pulled it up and over her head. Next, he removed her jeans and socks, exposing her black, thong panties, and then straightened up to work on taking off her bra. His desire for her evident, she reached out for his rigid flesh, dabbing her thumb in his precum and stroking his juices over his purple head. His eyes closed, his head rolled back, and he moaned a deep, guttural sound, vibrating through her body to shake her to her core. He belonged to her, with all his vulnerability for her to see, and she loved him all the more for it.

With his focus back on Catrina, he unhooked her bra, letting it fall to the floor to join their pile of clothes. Bending over and capturing one of her elongated nipples in his mouth, he suckled from her breast, while playfully pulling at the other nipple making both of them swollen and hard. She could never grow tired of his touch and the pure bliss he brought to her body.

Working his way down her form, he slid his hand between her legs and rubbed her pussy through her panties. She pushed herself against his hand, loving the sensation he created. When he pulled away, he brought his fingers to his lips and tasted her juices, which had soaked through the flimsy material.

"You taste so sweet," he said placing his hand on the side string of her panties and yanking hard, ripping them off her body.

An ache coursed through her snatch, as it throbbed with longing to be filled. "Oh, you naughty boy, ripping off my panties like an animal."

"Yes, I'm an animal for you." Immediately, he slipped his fingers into her shaved pussy, coating them with her essence. "I have something else I think you're going to like too." He brought the tips to her mouth, running them over each lip, then slipped them inside. As he pushed farther inside, she opened her mouth and sucked hungrily.

Since she'd never tasted her own juices before, she found this quite erotic. She tasted sweet and musky. Removing his fingers, he kissed her again, sucking on her top and bottom lip in turn. His hands moved back to her breasts, and he squeezed their fullness, moaning in her mouth. He dropped his head again to her tit and sucked, then rolled and flicked his tongue on her nipple.

His hands moved to her ass, and she felt his reluctance in releasing her breast. After lifting her onto the dresser, he spread her legs wide. He stood back, gazing at her body, appearing to take her in, his erection pointed straight for his goal.

"Please, Alex, take me now. I'm so ready for you."

Reaching her hand out for him, she moved first, pulling him to her, resting the swollen head of his cock against her pussy. She stroked him up and down her wet slit and guided him into her core.

Immediately, he began to thrust into her in a steady, strong rhythm.

"Oh God, you feel so good inside of me." Wrapping her legs around him, she pulled him deeper inside her body.

"Oh, Cat, you're so tight," he said as he pounded harder, held her tighter, and growled toward her. "Mine," rumbled from his throat.

Feeling his possession of her, she loved every second of it.

Their mutual passion bonded them with every thrust of his cock. He started to finger her clit as he continued to plunge deep into her cunt. "I want you to come for me, baby. I want to hear you scream your desire for me."

She'd been close to coming, but with his magic touch on her clit, he pushed her over the edge of reason. "Oh God...ah...yes!" she cried out as her body clenched around his cock causing him to follow close behind her.

"Yes...oh...baby!" he growled, holding her tighter against his body as he came deep in her snatch, filling her full of his cum.

They leaned against each other, their hearts pounding in rhythm together while they caught their breath in a lover's embrace. Catrina realized they belonged together, Alex suiting her perfectly.

He moved first, pulling away from her and helping her off the dresser. Leading her to her bed, he pushed the covers back and guided her to lie down in the cozy warmth of the mattress. Smiling, he leaned down and kissed her cheek. "I'll be right back."

Alex's retreat left Catrina alone with her thoughts. *I hope you understand, Phil. I love you, and I always will.* A feeling of relief and peace washed over her heart as if Phil approved of her new union and blessed it somehow.

A few minutes later, Alex came back into the room, still naked, and crawled into bed beside her. Pulling her into his arms, he held her like a precious gem in his warm embrace. Snuggling against him, she heard him snap his fingers a couple of times.

"What was that for?"

He looked at her innocently, as Dapple came running into the room and jumped on the bed.

"Hey, little guy, what are you doing here?" The kitten marched across the bed, and Catrina's body, to sit on Alex's chest.

"What's this?" Catrina asked, noticing a big red bow tied around Dapple's neck.

"I don't know. It's a mystery to me. Maybe he has something for you."

"This seems very suspicious. I think you two are in cahoots." She laughed as she pulled the willing kitty closer and untied the bow. Hidden in the folds of the ribbon, she noticed a large gold heart pendant with small diamond on one side and engraving on the back. She read the note aloud.

My Little Cat,
Here's to many more Valentine's Days together.
Love forever, Alex.

"This is so beautiful. Thank you so much."

"You're very welcome. I have the chain for it in my coat pocket. I didn't want to weigh Dapple down anymore than I already had. I meant what I said. I'm here forever. I'm yours, heart and soul if you want me."

"I couldn't ask for a better Valentine's Day present than you. I do feel bad, though. I didn't get you anything."

"I have everything I want right here," he said as he leaned over to kiss her and hug Dapple at the same time.

THE END

Forever Kind of Love
By
Sandy Sullivan

Chapter One

Valentine's Day sucked! Becky O'Rourke hated it with a passion. Hoping the one coming up in a few days would be different, only broke her heart even more. Ever since the last one turned out so badly, she decided the day wasn't worth much, all the mushiness of couples everywhere and God forbid she run into Emma, Brandon and Beau. Those three were the worst. Hugging and kissing each other—the guys fawning over their son. *Yuck!* Lucky for her, they didn't live in Red Rock anymore, only visiting several times a year. She missed her friend terribly, but Emma was happy in her relationship with her men and Becky adored seeing the love they shared even if she'd never have the same for herself.

The man she wanted didn't love her. Seth Reardon.

She hated him with every other breath from her body and loved him with the rest. Would she ever get over him? She didn't think so and all her father could do was say 'I told you so'.

Two summers ago she finally gave into his asking her out, much to the delight of Emma. They quickly fell in love—or she had anyway.

Every day he told her how much he cared about her and how much he looked forward to the day their relationship would blossom into a lifetime of love and happiness. She foolishly believed every word.

Until Valentine's Day last year.

They made a date for dinner and Seth said he planned something special for their day. Little did she know his something special meant breaking her heart.

She'd been waiting anxiously at home, dressed to the hilt with a brand new white flowing skirt and soft blue off one shoulder blouse, her mother's pearls around her neck and a diamond bracelet her father had given her for her sixteenth birthday, on her wrist. With her hair up in a soft upswept hairdo, light makeup and shiny lip gloss, she'd paced the living room watching the clock.

The soft knock on the door startled her and she glanced through the sheer blinds to see Seth standing on the porch. When she opened the door, she was shocked to see his hair mussed like he'd been running his hands through it, his eyes red-rimmed and his clothes wrinkled.

"Seth, what's wrong? You look terrible."

"Becky, we can't see each other anymore."

"What! Why?" she said, her throat closing to any other words.

"We just can't." He reached out like he wanted to touch her, but stopped halfway and then let his hand drop back to his side. "I'm sorry." He laid a single red rose on the bench against the railing of her porch and walked away.

For almost a year she'd avoided anything to do with Seth Reardon. She didn't go to community events if he would be there. The rodeo didn't happen for her anymore. Her nights were spent in front of her television cuddling her cat, Simon on her lap and wishing for something she couldn't have. All she wanted to know was why.

This Valentine's Day I'm done moping around after Mr. I-can't-see-you-anymore. The new vet in town, Marcus Milton had asked her out a time or two, but she'd always turned him down. Well, not anymore. In fact…

She picked up her phone and dialed his office.

"Doctor Milton's office. Can I help you?"

"Yes. Is there any way I can speak with Doctor Milton, please?"

"Is this in regards to a patient?" the receptionist asked.

"Well, uh…yes. Sort of," Becky said, wincing as she lied to the woman on the phone.

"Can I ask who is calling and I'll see if he's free."

"Becky O'Rourke."

"One moment please."

Elevator music started playing in her ear. Not unpleasant even though it wasn't her type of music. Good old country and rock were her favorites.

Give her some George Strait, AC/DC, Garth Brooks or Journey and she loved it.

"Hello, Becky?"

"Hi, Marcus," she replied.

"Is something wrong with Simon? You can bring him in right away if you need to."

"I'm sorry, Marcus. I kind of fibbed a little. Simon is fine, but I wasn't sure if your receptionist would let me talk to you if I told her it was personal."

"Personal?"

"I know you've asked me out a couple of times before and well, I'm sorry I turned you down. I wanted to see if you'd like to have dinner with me tonight?"

"Uh…sure. How about I pick you up at your house around six?"

"Great. I'll see you then."

After hanging up the phone, she let a small smile spread across her lips. She had a date! Even though Marcus didn't have Seth's rugged good looks, he definitely had handsome down. Chestnut colored hair and big blue eyes sure spun her wheels—when she wasn't thinking, lusting or drooling over Seth.

"Enough! Seth doesn't want me and I'm tired of waiting for him to change his damned mind. He made it clear there wasn't anything between us anymore when he walked away last year."

There. She'd convinced her mind if not her heart she'd gotten over Seth Reardon and would be moving on with her life. A great theory anyway.

To top it off, she planned to wear the same outfit she'd worn the night Seth broke her heart. That would show him. Not like he'd know it probably, but she felt better for doing something a little spiteful for the way he'd dumped her.

Two hours later, she stood dressed and ready. Her stomach felt like a thousand butterflies danced inside. A year was too long to wait to reenter the dating pool and too long to wait to get over Seth Reardon.

The doorbell chimed with a gay peal, announcing the arrival of her date. Six o'clock. Right on time. Seth had been forever late whenever they dated. *Enough. I'm not going to compare Marcus to Seth all damned night. Seth made his bed and now he can lie in it alone. At least I hope he's in it alone.*

When she opened the door, Marcus turned around and his eyes lit up with an appreciative gleam.

"Wow. You look great!"

"Thank you. Would you like to come in for a moment while I get my coat?"

"Sure," he replied, opening the screen and stepping inside the doorway. "Nice place."

"Again, thank you. I'll be right back." She spun around and headed for the coat closet to retrieve her jacket. The white skirt swirled around her legs making her feel feminine and pretty. Too bad Seth hadn't had the chance to appreciate it on her.

"Stop it!"

"Pardon?" Marcus said from several feet behind her.

"Sorry. It's nothing. I'm talking to myself." She spun around to face him with coat in hand.

"Simon looks healthy and happy." Marcus bent down to pet the cat entwining himself around Marcus' legs.

"Thanks. He's my baby, so he's spoiled rotten."

"Ah. Cats are such loveable creatures."

"Are you more of a cat person or dog person?"

He scratched the cat behind the ears and under the chin. "Not a fair question to ask a vet."

"Oh sorry."

"I'm teasing, Becky. I like both equally actually. They each have their own personalities and quirks. Dogs are fun, playful and exuberant where cats are mellow, self-sufficient and cuddly."

"True." She struggled to pull the coat around her shoulders and he grabbed the back to help her. "Thanks."

"When did you break your wrist?" he asked, nodding to the cast on her left arm.

"Two weeks ago. I fell on some ice on my front walk during the last snow storm."

"I bet it hurt like the devil."

"Yeah, but it's better now. It's just a nuisance having the cast on, but at least it's not my dominant hand."

"You'll have to let me sign it."

The grin he gave her warmed her heart. He really was a nice guy and cute…but he wasn't Seth.

* * * *

Whiskey. I need a good shot of whiskey. He, Seth Reardon was a pussy. He'd let the best thing in his life walk away a little less than a year ago over what? His own insecurities. After a talk with his best friend, Joe Collier, he'd come to realize he didn't have anything to offer a girl like Becky. The bar paid his bills, but didn't leave a lot extra afterward. He lived above the bar in a small apartment. Nothing fancy. Becky owned her home. Had a good job and had a dad who loved her. He had no one anymore. His father died a few years ago. His mother ran out on them when he was a baby, leaving his dad to raise him alone. Seth wondered if he even knew how to love anyone. Surely, he didn't. His dad never said 'I love you'. Not once. The bar was his mistress and his life until his death and now it had become Seth's.

The clank of the bottle against the rim of the glass seemed loud in the quiet bar as he poured himself a shot and threw it into the back of his throat. The burn of the whiskey calmed the ache in his chest. Drinking had become a staple for him lately. He hated himself for giving into the booze, but nothing could stem the self-loathing he felt for breaking Becky's heart. Tonight, he could drown his sorrows since the bar didn't open on Tuesday's and he had no place to be except in his apartment alone with his television and the bottle.

A car door slammed, drawing his attention to the window. Grabbing his glass, he wandered over to see what might be going on. Trouble outside would bring the cops and he vaguely wondered if Laurel Dunn might be working tonight. The wife of Becky's best friend's brother could be ruthless when it came to drinking and driving. Luckily, he wasn't driving anywhere.

With the glass to his lips, he peered outside noticing a newer Ford pickup truck parked next to the curb. One of the fanciest restaurants in town sat two blocks down from where he stood. Apparently, their parking lot was full or the cheap bastard in the truck didn't want to pay for valet.

"Figures," he grumbled, tipping the tumbler up and draining the contents in one fiery gulp. "Damn rot gut."

Shit! It can't be.

Sure enough the love of his life stepped out of the truck and drew her coat closer to her body. Pressing closer to the glass, he recognized her red hair gleaming in the light overhead as she smiled at the new vet in town. *Damn it!* Seeing her smile at someone else twisted his gut into a knot. He'd let her go. He knew that, but it didn't make seeing her dating any easier. He hadn't seen her except from a distance, in almost a year to the day. Valentine's Day last year, to be exact.

Before he could stop, he stood at the open door of his bar as the couple walked arm-and-arm toward him.

"Hi you two."

Her steps came to a faltering stop. "Seth."

"I don't believe we've met. I'm Marcus Milton, the new vet."

"Seth Reardon. I own the bar."

"Ah. I haven't frequented your establishment yet."

"I don't believe you have, Doc. I know everyone who comes into my bar." His gaze never left Becky. "It's good to see you, Becky."

"You too, Seth. How've you been?"

"Good."

"We should go, Becky. We have reservations at the restaurant."

"Oh. Yes, of course."

"I guess I'll see you around," Seth said, not quite ready to let her leave.

"Probably not. We don't seem to run into each other very often anymore." She tucked a piece of hair behind her ear.

"True."

The urge to draw her into his arms and kiss her until she yielded under his touch again—like she used to—almost drove him to his knees.

She glanced back one last time as Marcus led her down the sidewalk.

The door moved easily under his hand as he stepped back inside the bar and slammed it shut. "God damn it!" The glass shattered when he threw it against the far wall and dropped his head back on his shoulders. Nothing but the rough beams of the ceiling above him, stared back. His eyes burned from unshed tears. He needed her. Wanted her with every fiber of his being, but he couldn't have her. He wasn't good enough for her.

Maybe you should have given her that choice. You never told her why you broke it off.

"Shut up!"

* * * *

"Are you all right?" Marcus asked as they were led to their table.

"I'm fine."

Once they had been seated, he took her hand in his. "What's the history between you and Seth?"

"Nothing, why?"

He shook his head sadly. "Come on, Becky. The longing in both of your eyes took my breath away. I hope someday to have a love like that."

"It doesn't matter, Marcus. He broke up with me almost a year ago," she replied, grabbing her menu and flipping it open. Seeing Seth made her want to cry. Her chest hurt and she knew it was from her heart breaking inside. *Damn the man! Why did he have to ruin my date?*

"Did he tell you why?"

"No. I guess I wasn't good enough for him or something."

"Not good enough? If that's his excuse, then he doesn't deserve you." Marcus picked up his own menu and glanced over the top at her. "We'll have a nice dinner and I'll take you home."

"I want this to be a regular date. I'm not letting Seth Reardon ruin it anymore than he already has."

"If you didn't care about him, he wouldn't have ruined it for you."

She slapped the menu down on the table as anger swept through her. "All right. I care about him. Okay? It doesn't matter what I feel. He doesn't want me. He's made his lack of feelings perfectly clear and I'm tired of sitting at home alone. Now, if you'd rather not finished this date, you can take me home."

"Whoa! Hang on here. I never said I didn't want to finish our date. I'd love to learn more about you and maybe someday you can move on without him if he doesn't return your affection. I just wanted to make sure you knew I was aware of your feelings for him," Marcus said, taking her hand again. "Who knows? Maybe we can push him to decide one way or another."

"I'm not following you."

"Do you want him to either cut loose and let you go completely or declare his true feelings?"

"I want him to love me like I love him."

"Let's give him something to stew over then, shall we?" Marcus brought her hand to his lips, smiled a teasing little grin and then kissed the back of her hand.

She wasn't exactly sure what he was doing until he whispered against her flesh, "Seth just walked in. Alone." She moved to look, but he stopped her. "No. Look at me. Think of me as Seth and give me your best loving look."

Marcus' face morphed into Seth's and the teasing little grin he loved to give her before he kissed her silly. The twinkle in his dark eyes melted her insides like butter in the hot summer sun. *"I love you, Becky."* Seth's dark, rich voice washed over her like a warm, fuzzy blanket.

"Yeah, perfect," Marcus said, breaking the spell. "He's taken a seat at the bar, but he's watching us in the mirror. Whatever you do, think of me as him and he'll be eating his heart out inside of thirty minutes."

She did exactly what Marcus said and imagined him as Seth. Using Marcus like this didn't sit well with her, but he seemed to want to play matchmaker like Emma did two summers ago when she forced the two of them to talk out their differences. Once she knew a relationship with Seth wouldn't give her father a heart attack, she'd embraced it and the attraction with both arms wide open. The eight months following were the best of her life. She'd fallen so deeply in love with Seth and thought he had with her too. The break off had been such a shock, she didn't eat for days, missed work and wanted to die.

Now, she was about to let him hurt her all over again.

Chapter Two

Son of a bitch! Watching Becky with Marcus tore at his gut and his heart. He wanted her—no needed her and there she sat looking so lost in love with that vet, he wanted to gag.

The way he kissed her hand and she melted on the chair made him want to punch something. Preferably her new boyfriend. How dare she find someone else. How long had they been dating? Months, probably. Hell, she'd more than likely started dating the guy right after he broke it off with her.

Marcus stood and leaned over Becky. The kiss he planted on what appeared to be her lips, made Seth growl low in his throat as jealousy seared his heart. The next moment when Marcus slid his hands around Becky's waist and held her close as they danced, Seth could have thrown up had there been anything in his stomach besides alcohol.

He hadn't moved on and found anyone else. The town knew he wasn't good enough for any of the ladies of Red Rock and so did he. Owning a bar didn't qualify as a good catch around here. Several of the town's families including the Weston's and Dunn's were founding fathers of the town and a guy like him wouldn't be welcome. Even Becky's father, the local preacher, didn't like him. Hated him in fact because of his Jewish heritage. Even if he wasn't a practicing Jew.

Well to hell with them all. Seth Reardon didn't back down from a fight and if he had to fight for something, he'd damned well fight for Becky's love. Yes, he loved her. Had loved her for two years.

He hadn't thanked Emma for sticking her nose in their business, but he should have. The summer she'd given him a virtual kick in the butt to talk to Becky, gave him the courage to go after the one woman he'd admired from afar for too long.

Enough's enough. He did own a bar and it paid the bills. He might not have a lot to offer a girl like Becky, but he had his love. If it wasn't good enough, then she had to tell him so.

He slid off the barstool and stumbled. *Too much to drink. I'd better wait to talk to her until I'm sober.* After a quick glance in her direction and noticing her continued lovey-dovey look at Marcus, he made his way out the door and down the sidewalk to the back door of his apartment. The stairs mocked him with silent laughter as he sighed and methodically pulled his now weary body up each step and fished his keys out of his jeans pocket. A good night's sleep would do him good, even though he hadn't gotten one of those in months.

The next morning, he woke still dressed and lying diagonal across his bed. How the hell he managed to even make it there, he wasn't sure.

His mouth tasted pasty like he'd been snoring, which he probably had. He rolled over and stared at the ceiling for a moment as images of the night before flashed through his foggy brain.

Running into Becky and Marcus outside the bar. Following them to the restaurant and mooning over her like a lovesick fool in the mirror while she smiled, laughed and simpered over the new vet. The conclusion he'd come to. Make it right or leave her alone. He had to do something. This situation was out of control and he either needed to move on or come clean with her over why he'd broken up with her. The thought of getting back together with her left him almost giddy.

First a shower and then he had plans to make. Wouldn't it be fitting to get back together with her one year exactly to the day he'd stopped seeing her? All he could hope for was she hadn't moved on without him and the scene last night with Marcus was a mistake.

After he pulled himself up off the bed, he stumbled to his feet and held his head. Damn it. Whiskey hurt the day after. He hoped he hadn't made a complete fool of himself the night before in front of Becky, but he couldn't quite remember everything. The one thing he did remember drove him crazy. The looks Becky gave Marcus. He wanted her looking only at him with those big green eyes and loving smile.

He headed into the bathroom for a quick shower. Once he'd completed that task, he could concentrate on what he had to do to win Becky back.

The warm water felt invigorating as it pounded against his back and shoulders even in the small enclosure. He always imagined showering with Becky although they'd never got to try it out. Nothing better than shower sex on the spur of the moment.

His cock hardened at the thought. Her warm mouth would envelope the head, sucking softly until she swirled her tongue around and around. The rough pad of her tongue would trace the veins running along the underside until she slowly engulfed the entire length of him in the hot cavern of her mouth. Suck, swallow. Suck, swallow.

Ah hell!

Unable to lose the image now, he wrapped his fist around his cock and moved it up and down. This had become a ritual in the last year. The pictures of Becky on her hands and knees as he fucked her from behind, tortured him day and night. More of her on her knees sucking his cock until he squirted every last drop of cum down her throat. Yes, they'd been intimate.

The first time they'd made love came back in sharp clarity.

They'd dated for six months before giving into the lust and attraction screaming between them. She hadn't been a virgin, but he hadn't anticipated it anyway.

A candlelight dinner, soft music and flower petals everywhere set the mood. She'd actually seduced him rather than him seducing her. When he'd shown up at her house, she was wearing a soft green wrap around dress and no shoes.

She'd looked so beautiful, she took his breath away. The dress matched her eyes and set off her red hair. The light behind her reflected the gold highlights like fire around her head when she'd opened the door to his knock.

"We're staying in tonight. My treat. Dinner will be ready in about fifteen minutes."

"What's the occasion?"

"Nothing special." She shrugged and then smiled. "Maybe our six month anniversary or something."

"Has it been six months already?"

She smacked his arm. "Like you didn't know. You've been hinting at it for weeks." With his hand in her grasp, she pulled him inside and shut the door. Moments later, he found himself against the door with her lips on his.

Damn, could she kiss. Her lips tasted sweet with a little bite from a soda she'd drank before he got there. Taking control of the situation, he quickly reversed their positions and pressed her hard against the wooden panel. The attraction between them sizzled in the air and had from the moment he'd laid eyes on her. She released a small groan into his mouth when his hand found her breast. God, he wanted her. Needed her.

After he lifted his head and stared into her eyes, he said, "Not now, Becky."

"I want you, Seth."

"I know. I'm right there, but I want it to be special. Not just a wham-bam-thank-you-ma'am. You're extraordinary and what I feel for you can't be described in simple words."

"What do you feel for me?"

"I think I'm falling in love with you."

"Good. Me too."

"What?" he asked, afraid he hadn't heard her correctly.

"I'm falling in love with you too, and I want us to make love. Have sex. Do the horizontal mambo. You know." Her hands made quick work of the buttons down the front of his shirt.

With a heavy sigh, he stepped back. "After dinner…maybe."

"Maybe? Don't you want to make love to me, Seth?"

"More than anything, but we need to slow down."

"Why?" she asked, returning to her task of undressing him as she talked.

"Damn it, Becky. Stop!"

Her eyes widened and her face drained of all color. "I'm sorry. I guess I shouldn't be so forward."

"God no, sweetheart. It's not that. I'm just so fucking horny right now, I could chew nails and having you all over me is driving me crazy." He framed her face with his hands. "I want you so bad, it's killing me, but I want this to be special, baby. You've already started with the dinner, flower petals and all this. Let's just take it a little slower. Okay?"

The tears on her lashes about did him in, but he breathed a sigh of relief when she nodded and stepped back.

"We'll do this your way."

Dinner seemed strained even though he tried to lighten it up by teasing her and joking with her. The lines around her mouth told him how tense she held herself waiting for him to give her the signal it would be okay for them to make love now. Although, he wasn't sure now was the best time.

"Don't you dare change your mind, Seth Reardon. I won't wait anymore. I've been trying to get you to make love to me for weeks, but you keep pushing me away. If you don't want to, just say so and we'll move on without each other. But let me tell you one thing. I'm getting laid tonight with or without you," Becky said, before she jumped to her feet and grabbed her plate.

Well now. She's got a bit of a fire under her ass apparently.

"Oh, we're gonna make love, Becky O'Rourke." He slowly climbed to his feet and followed her into the small kitchen. When he touched her shoulder, she spun around seemingly startled by his proximity. "In fact, make sure the table is cleared and wiped down, baby. Because I'm gonna take you on it."

"I'm no virgin afraid of rough sex."

"Good. I won't have to play nice then because I like it a bit on the rough side." His lips latched onto hers in a bone melting kiss. Her lips parted in a gasp and he drove his tongue inside her mouth to taste and explore. The perpetual hard-on he'd been sporting for six months ached for release in some other method besides his fist as he wrapped his hand in her hair and tipped her head back.

After several moments, he lifted his head and stared down into her eyes. "Get this cleaned up and I'll be right back." He had something to retrieve from his truck.

* * * *

The day after the dinner with Marcus and pretending he was Seth, Becky stood by the window in her house letting the memories swamp her. Thoughts about the first time she and Seth made love came rushing back as her heart ached for the man who'd dashed her hopes of an everlasting love with the words 'I can't see you anymore.'

He'd come over for a normal dinner date with her, but she'd decided earlier in the day seduction was her plan. Candlelight dinner, soft music, and rose petals set the mood, but he'd been so damned stubborn about it, she'd almost given up on him ever making love to her.

From the moment he'd walked in through the front door, she'd taunted, flirted and did anything and everything to flip his switch.

What the hell was she thinking teasing him? Her whole body quivered with anticipation. Seth didn't come across as the forceful type, but all this tough talk had her so hot, she thought she might combust.

She quickly cleared the table and put all the dishes in the sink. Without a second thought, she grabbed some of the rose petals she's strewn about the living room, throwing them on the dining room table. If he planned on taking her on the hard surface, she wanted to make sure it was at least a little romantic.

"Romantic hell. I want him to take me hard and fast." Her stomach turned over just thinking about his cock buried in her pussy or her ass. It had been a long time since she'd had anal sex and unfortunately for her sometimes guys didn't go for it.

"Ready?" he asked from the doorway.

"For?"

"Toys, baby, toys."

Her stomach dropped. "What kind of toys?"

"Vibrators, butt plugs, lots of lube?"

She sighed knowing tonight would blow her mind. "All of the above?"

"Strip."

"Yes, Sir." Nervous now, she worked the tie at her waist on the right and then loosened the dress across the bodice.

Seth leaned against the back of the couch, his treasure sack clutched tight in his hand as she let the front of her dress fall to her waist. Never having stripped in front of a man before, she wasn't quite sure what to do next, but the appreciation in his eyes gave her courage. She slipped the rest of her dress down over her hips, taking her silky pants along with it. Standing in front of him naked as the day she was born made her self-conscious of her thicker thighs and too round butt.

"Well?" she asked with her hands spread wide.

"Magnificent. You're so beautiful you take my breath away."

"Are you going to strip too?"

"Eventually, baby. For now, I want to look. A man likes to look, you know."

She bit her lip and tried to calm the nervous butterflies in her stomach.

"Turn."

"What?"

"Turn around. I want to see the back."

"But I have a big butt," she said as she turned her back toward him.

The sting of his bare hand against her flesh startled her into a yelp.

"You have the nicest ass I've seen anywhere and I'll not have you talking bad about the body I want so much I hurt." His arms snacked around her waist and he drew her back against his chest. "I love you, Becky, but make no mistake. I like my sex with a bite. If you aren't up to it, let me know now."

Her heart pounded so loud in her ears, she almost didn't hear his words. "Rough?"

"I won't hurt you." He walked her toward the table. "Lie on your stomach."

The dining room table felt cool against her heated flesh. She couldn't see Seth and it made her a bit nervous. She could feel his jean clad thighs brushing hers.

"First things first. Safe word. What do you want to use?"

"Safe word?"

"Something like red will do."

"Red is fine, but what do I need it for?"

"In case things get too much for you either physically or mentally, but don't use it lightly because if you use it, everything stops and I go home."

"No!"

"Good. Ever had a butt plug?"

"No."

"Ever had a man in your ass?"

"Yes."

"Did you like it?"

She wasn't sure if she could admit the naughtiness of wanting a man's cock in the dark, forbidden place or not. His hand came down on her butt cheek again. "Ouch."

"Did you like it?"

"Yes, all right. I liked it. A lot."

"Such a naughty girl for a preacher's daughter."

"Don't mock me, Seth."

"Sorry, baby. It just surprises me."

"It shouldn't. My daddy doesn't know I've even had sex. He thinks I'm still a virgin."

"Personally, I'm glad you're not." She heard the distinctive sound of the cap on the lubricant bottle shortly before the cold, wet slide of it hit her behind. "I'm going to put this plug inside you. Push back when you've got the urge."

The miniscule beginning of a burn started in her rectum as Seth pushed the plug slowly through her anal muscles. A small hiss escaped her lips.

"Okay?"

"Yeah. It's been a while."

"Nice to know."

Soon, the plug slid past the widest part as she felt the base against her bottom.

"I want to touch you."

"Not this time." His finger glanced over her clit and then plunged inside her pussy.

"Ahhhh!"

"A little horny are we?" he asked, working his finger in and out.

"A lot horny, Seth. Please."

"Please what?"

"Fuck me. I need you deep."

The crinkling sound of a condom wrapper reached her ear and she braced herself with her hands on the other side of the table for his plunge. But he didn't take her right away. "What are you waiting for?"

He swirled his fingers in her juices and spread them around and around her clit. "I don't want to rush this."

"We can do it again slow in a few minutes. Right now I need you to fuck me, damn it!"

"I'm letting you get away with mouthing off this time, but rest assured, baby, it's only because I can't hold back anymore."

A scream ripped from her throat as he grabbed her hips and rammed his cock home. "Yes, yes, yes."

Chapter Three

The shower had grown cooler by the time Seth lost his grip on his climax and cum squirted up his stomach. He sagged against the wall, breathing hard and shaking his head to clear his foggy brain. Coming that hard always took it out of him even if they didn't happen very often and a lot less since he'd broke up with Becky.

Things were gonna change if he had anything to say about it. To hell with her and Marcus. She belonged to Seth and by God, they were going to be together if it killed him and it just might. Proving to her he could and would make her the happiest woman on the planet, might be difficult since he didn't have a lot. Hell, her daddy's place was fancier than his little apartment above the bar. He didn't care whether the church supplied her daddy his home or not. The large cottage next to the church with its abundant flowerbeds, climbing ivy and bubbling fountain screamed homey far beyond anything Seth could give her.

He finished washing his hair and body as the doubts resurfaced again.
What if she doesn't want me back?
What if I can't make her happy?
What if she doesn't love me anymore?
What if she's in love with Marcus now?

"Enough! I have to give her the chance to tell me." He grabbed a towel and dried off as he walked toward his room. The queen-sized four poster bed took up most of the bedroom, but he had to have a longer bed being over six feet in height. To share it with Becky had been the best thing in his life and he'd screwed it up.

"No more. To hell with her dad and his condescending attitude. To hell with us having a lot. If we have love, then it'll be enough." He quickly pulled on a pair of jeans, a long-sleeved shirt and grabbed some socks and his boots. The errands he needed to run couldn't wait this close to Valentine's Day. The flower shop might be out of roses and he might not be able to get reservations at the restaurant housed inside the hotel. He snapped his fingers and grinned. His credit card might get maxed out, but Becky would be worth it.

Grabbing his cell phone, he dialed the hotel. "I need to make reservations for a suite for Friday."

"I'm sorry Sir, but the entire hotel is booked except the honeymoon suite."

"Perfect. I'll take it."

"It's two hundred eighty-nine dollars, plus tax, sir."

He groaned and pulled out his credit card. "Fine. Here's my credit card number. I'll also need a bottle of champagne and several dozen roses. Can you handle the order?"

"Certainly, sir."

"Excellent."

"Celebration, sir?"

"I'm hoping so, yes," he said as he pulled out the diamond solitaire from his pocket where it's been sitting since this time last year.

"Very good, sir. We'll see you on Friday."

Now, what to wear. Tux? Suit? Jeans and a flannel shirt? She'd probably kill him if he got too fancy and if he wore jeans, she'd definitely kill him.

He had to figure out how to get her to the hotel.

"Emma!"

With cell phone in hand, he grabbed a beer and took a seat at his dining room table. His hands shook as he found Emma's phone number and stared at it for several minutes before he hit talk.

"Hello?"

"Emma?"

"Yes, who's this?"

"Seth Reardon."

Click.

Fuck! She hung up on me!

He dialed again and got voicemail. "Emma, please. I know you're probably majorly pissed off at me for what I did to Becky, but I need your help. I'm begging here. I want her back. I love her and I don't care if she's dating Marcus Milton or not. I have a plan to win her back or try to. I even have an engagement ring I want to give her. Please call me back."

He waited several moments, and then his phone rang. "Emma?"

"What's your plan, Seth? I'll warn you, if you hurt her again, I'll personally break both of your legs or have one of Brandon's bodyguards do it for me."

"I made a mistake," he replied, running his hands through his hair.

"No shit."

"I let someone talk me into believing I wasn't good enough for her. I don't have a lot, Emma. You know that."

"She wanted you, Seth. Not what you have or don't have."

"I could hardly provide for her."

"Ever heard of a two income household?" Emma asked, irritation clear in her voice and he couldn't blame her.

The stupidity of what he'd done made his stomach hurt. "Yeah, but I was supposed to take care of her."

"Listen, dumbass. She loved you. Still does from what I hear when I talk to her. And what's this about someone named Marcus?"

"I saw her out with him last night. They had dinner together."

"Must be the new vet she mentioned, but I didn't think she'd said yes."

"Apparently she did. They made it look like they've been dating a while."

"Not that I know of."

"How are you, Brandon and Beau doing?"

"Good. We're expecting again. June baby this time."

"I'm sure your little boy is growing like crazy."

"Yes, he is and Beau already has him on horseback. Silly man. He's only two."

"It's a guy thing, I'm sure. Brandon will probably be teaching him to play guitar soon too."

"Already is. We bought him a smaller one for his hands, but he'll be tall like his daddies."

Misty eyed, he said, "I'm happy for you, Emma. Y'all make such a cute threesome."

"I never thought I'd be this happy, Seth and I hope you and Becky can get things straightened out."

"That brings me back to why I called. I need your help getting her to the hotel. I've booked a room with champagne and roses, but I'm not sure how to get her there. It's the honeymoon suite even."

"Huh. Let me think a moment. It's not going to be easy. She's been telling me for weeks how she plans to stay in and eat her way through two gallons of ice cream by herself."

"What about you telling her you'll meet her at the hotel?"

"On Valentine's Day, Seth? She'll never buy me leaving the guys on Valentine's Day to spend it with her. Besides, she knows Brandon and Beau have planned something special. We even have a sitter to take care of our son so we can have some alone time."

"I *really* don't need to hear about it, Emma."

"Sorry, but it's the truth." After a long pause, she said, "I've got it. Give me Marcus' number. I need to talk to him."

"The enemy?" he asked as he looked up the vet's number.

"Only if he's really interested. Let me find out what's between them and I'll see what I can do. I'll call you back in a little while."

After he hung up, he drank his beer and paced. He tried to watch television, but nothing could hold his attention for long. He even tried deciding what to wear, but his thoughts kept going back to the last time he'd made love to Becky in his bed— only a week before he'd broken off their relationship. *Damn Joe anyway.*

He jumped when his phone rang an hour later.

"It's all set," Emma said. "She'll be at the hotel at five."

"What did you say?"

"Never mind. Just be ready. It seems Marcus is all about getting you two back together."

"I didn't tell you the number though."

"I know which one is the honeymoon suite, Seth. My brother is a co-owner of the thing and I spent part of my honeymoon there."

"Great. I've already closed the bar for the evening since it's usually slow anyway. People in Red Rock don't want to spend Valentine's Day at the bar."

He heard a heavy sigh.

"This is your one shot. If you don't convince her you love her, I can't help you anymore. I won't risk my friendship with her to save your ass again. Understood?"

"Perfectly. You're the best, Emma."

"Just remember what I said. Hurt her again and I'll break both your legs."

"Got it. Talk to you later."

"Bye."

* * * *

Soft music played as the cooler air hit Becky in the face when she rushed through the double glass doors of the Mill House Hotel. Emma wasn't very clear on what the problem was just that Marcus wanted to meet her here in suite twenty-one-twelve. She needed to dress nice and wear perfume? Odd. She figured Marcus would have called himself, but Emma said he was embarrassed about not calling her himself after their date and wanted to make it up to her.

This whole thing sounded strange, but the call had come in from Emma not more than a few hours ago, leaving her not much time or choice in the matter.

The short black dress with the elbow length sleeves and full skirt swirled around her. The black mid length jacket she wore covered everything except her shapely legs and peep-toe shoes. She hoped it wasn't too much or too slinky for whatever Marcus had planned.

Maybe he'd changed his mind about wanting me together with Seth again. After the other night at the restaurant, he'd been the perfect gentleman. Didn't even kiss me goodnight.

The elevator dinged as it arrived at the ground floor. The bellman inside asked what floor and when she told him the room number she needed, he smiled a sly kind of a smile and pushed the button.

This whole evening was turning out really weird.

"Here you are, ma'am."

"Thank you. Can you point me where—"

"Second door on the left at the end of the hall. There are only four suites on this floor. Can't miss it."

She remembered Emma staying in one of these rooms after her joining ceremony to Brandon and Beau. Even though she'd never seen the inside of one, she knew they were luxurious.

After she found the correct room, she raised her hand and knocked softly calling out Marcus' name.

The door opened and Marcus held the door open for her. "Come in."

"What's going on, Marcus?"

"Alone time, sweetheart."

"Marcus, you know how I feel about Seth. This isn't right. I thought we agreed on—"

"We did," he replied, and then kissed her cheek. "Enjoy your evening and don't hate me for this."

Marcus disappeared out the door, leaving her to stand in the middle of a candlelit room with six doses roses scattered in vases around the area. Brandon's new hit single, "Forever Kind of Love" played softly in the background and Becky wished Seth could understand the concept of the type of love Brandon, Emma and Beau have.

A table with fine china and silver domes sat to the left. Whatever food sat underneath smelled wonderful as the scents drifted to her nose. A single red rose lay across a plate with an envelope. Her name scrawled in familiar handwriting swam before her eyes.

Her hands shook when she reached for the note.

Dear Becky,
I'm sorry I had to do this in such a sneaky manner, but I couldn't bring
myself to crawl back to you until now.
I love you with all of my heart and I have to apologize for how I treated you.
I never felt good enough for a woman like you, but I've come to realize
loving you should be enough.

"You have my heart and soul and always have." Seth's voice reached her ears as she read his words on the page. "Can you ever forgive me and love me again?"

Tears rolled down her cheeks and his face blurred when she lifted her head to see him standing outlined against the bank of glass overlooking the town of Red Rock below.

"I never stopped, Seth."

He moved closer. "I did the stupidest thing ever when I walked away from you. I didn't think I had enough to give you."

"All I wanted was your love."

"I can't give you a big house like Emma has or fancy cars—"

She stopped his words with her fingers against his lips. "If we have each other, it's enough. Someday we can buy another house or whatever. Being with you is all I ever wanted."

He kissed her fingertips, and then placed her hand on his chest near his heart. "You've owned this heart of mine for a long time. I don't ever want you to give it back."

"And you own mine forever."

"I want to make love to you. Right here, right now, but there is something I need to do first."

"What?"

He dropped down on one knee and pulled out the diamond ring. "Becky, will you marry me?"

She licked her lips and laughed. "Of course, I'll marry you. I love you."

"I love you too," he said, as he slipped the ring on her left hand, and then kissed her with so much passion, it took her breath away.

The moment she sighed, his tongue dove inside her mouth to tangle with hers. Their mouths fused and their hands explored.

She needed him to touch her in places long denied physical contact.

After she pulled her mouth free, she moaned, "Seth, please. I need you."

He took both of her hands and clasped them behind her back. "We should eat dinner before it gets cold."

"Seriously?"

"Anticipation makes it better, baby. You know that."

"Damn you."

His free hand came down on her butt. "Do it again."

"I forgot how much you enjoy spanking. I'll need to punish you some other way if you keep mouthing off."

"Did you bring toys?"

"Your favorites."

"Awfully sure of yourself weren't you?"

"Yes, after Marcus told me what you two pulled at the restaurant the other night."

"I wanted you to love me again."

He ran one finger down her cheek. "I never stopped, baby. I was just too blind to see our love could be enough to start with and we could build on the rest as we go along."

"I wish you would have talked to me instead of shutting me out." She huffed and pulled at her wrists, but he wasn't letting go.

"I'm a man. It's what men do, but I'll do my best to talk things out from now on."

"Are you going to make love to me or talk all night?"

"Just for that comment, we're going to eat first."

"Seth, wait. Please. I'm sorry, Sir. It's been so long."

"How about if I give you a little something to hold you until you get my cock in your ass?"

Her pussy throbbed and twitched at his words. She needed him so badly she forced herself not to rub her legs together to relieve the pressure. "Please."

He released one wrist, but kept a hold on the other until he had pulled her into the area where the bed lay. Dozens of rose petals were strewn across the bedspread.

"How pretty."

"All for you. Now strip."

Within moments she had her dress on the floor, her bra flipped over the headboard and her underwear around her ankles.

"Nice, baby." He waggled his eyebrows and crooked his finger. "Come here."

When she stepped close enough he could reach her, he grabbed her around the waist and tossed her on the bed amongst the petals.

"Wha—"

"I told you I'd help you out, but if you don't be quiet, I won't."

She zipped her lips closed and he laughed.

"That's my girl. Open," he said, tapping the inside of her thighs before he settled himself between her legs.

A quick lick over her clit had her moaning in ecstasy. The moment he sucked it between his lips, she almost came undone, but getting her off wasn't going to be quite so easy. *The slight relief I get from my vibrator would stall any climax I could have—Oh Hell!* Her whole body shook from the intense climax washing over her so fast she barely had time to breath.

"Damn, baby. I don't think I've ever made you come that quick before."

"God, Seth!" she screamed when he drove two fingers into her pussy, triggering another climax before the first one even finished.

Moments later, she felt the head of his cock at her entrance.

"I...thought we were going to eat first," she managed to say between panting breaths.

"I can't wait. I need you. Turn over."

"But—"

He quickly flipped her on her stomach. "I need your ass, baby."

"Lube?"

"Honey, you're so wet, I don't need lube."

"Fuck me then, Seth."

He eased the head of his cock through her slick juices, and then pushed against the tight ring of muscles at her ass.

"Oh, God, yes."

"Easy, baby."

"Fuck easy. Do it!"

She wanted it hard. No one had been in the dark passage of her ass since he'd been there the last time.

The whimpers she released told him she needed this as badly as he did. Her sighs would tell him she wanted this and her cries of ecstasy would tell him he'd better hurry up or she'd come again without him.

The moment his cock eased all the way inside, she forced her butt back against him and ground her ass against his pelvis.

"Please, Seth. I can't stand it."

He grabbed her hips and growled, "Hold on."

The slick slide of his cock in and out of her ass had them both on edge within seconds.

"Yes!"

Her pussy and ass muscles twitched and convulsed around him, wringing his own climax from deep inside with a satisfying groan. He collapsed onto her back, barely keeping from squishing her with his weight.

When he eased his cock from her ass, they both moaned and then sighed.

"I missed you."

"I missed you too," she said, her words muffled in the comforter on the bed. "I love you, Seth."

"I love you, Becky, and I'll never be so stupid as to walk away from you again. We'll talk everything out." He rolled beside her and traced her spine with his fingertips. "And we'll never go to bed angry. Promise?"

"I promise." She wiggled over onto her back, pushed the hair from her eyes and said, "When can I tell Emma?"

"She already knows."

"She does?"

"Yep. She helped me plan getting you over here with the help of Marcus."

"Well she doesn't know about the wedding, right?"

"Nope."

"Then can I call her?"

"Tomorrow. Tonight's our night for our forever kind of love."

The End

About The Authors

Sable Hunter

Sable Hunter writes erotic romances that run the gamut from cowboys to New Orleans witches to Texas good old boys that play football one day and ride bulls the next. She grew up in south Louisiana along the mysterious bayous where the Spanish moss hangs thick over the dark waters. The culture of Louisiana has shaped her outlook on life and has made its way into her paranormal romances where the supernatural is entirely normal. Presently, Sable lives in Texas and spends most of her time in wild and wonderful Austin. In the spring, her home sits in a field of bluebonnets.

While writing takes up a lot of her time, Sable also loves to cook Cajun, Creole and Tex-Mex. She is passionate about animals and has been known to charm creatures from a one ton bull to a family of raccoons. For fun, Sable has been known to haunt cemeteries and battlefields armed with night vision cameras and digital recorders hunting proof that love survives beyond the grave.

She writes for Secret Cravings Publishing and has several books coming out in the next year.

Cynthia Arsuaga

Cynthia resides in Orlando, Florida, the land of magic, surrounded by the treasured gems in her life, a caring, loving husband, dutiful and loyal daughter, and precious, delightful granddaughter. Oh and not to forget her mischievous Yorkshire terrier, Thumper.

Cynthia was a "Navy Brat" calling a different port home every couple of years—from Southern California, to Boston, to Virginia, to Florida. She developed wandering feet and diverse interests, and passionately incorporates those experiences into her stories, bringing characters to life, and eloquently sharing the vivid images of her mind with her audience.

Cynthia worked as a real estate broker for over twenty years before retiring to Florida. Until recently, then she turned to writing to stretch her creative muscle. Those ideas of faraway places and quirky characters lay dormant for years and finally demanded their story be told.

Cynthia plans on putting some mileage on those wandering feet and travel to exotic locations in the coming years. So look for the journeys to be expressed in the future.

Dana Littlejohn

Dana Littlejohn was born in Brooklyn, New York during a major snowstorm at a late night Christmas party. A trip to Indianapolis to visit a friend led her to her awesome husband Johnny and Indiana became her home. She spends the day at a nine to five at the hospital and every other moment writing. Her main goal in life is to be discovered as author extraordinaire so she can take her laptop to the white sand beaches of the Caribbean to write and drink Mai Tai's!

Daisy Dunn

Daisy Dunn considers herself a prairie girl, having lived most of her life in Winnipeg, Manitoba, Canada. She lives with the love of her life, who is also her common law partner and best friend.

Daisy is a hopeless romantic. She fell in love with reading romance novels at sixteen years of age when she read her first one. She was thoroughly hooked and hasn't stopped reading romance since.

Daisy always wanted to write, but life has a nasty habit of getting in the way of personal goals. Well, life finally stepped aside, and Daisy has started following her passion of writing erotic romances. Daisy's favorite genre to write is Paranormal, but she is not limited to it. She also writes erotic romances in Fantasy, Contemporary, and Cougar and is hoping to tackle Time Travel, Western and Ménage someday soon.

Sandy Sullivan

Sandy Sullivan is a romance author, who, when not writing, spends her time with her husband Shaun on their farm in middle Tennessee. She loves to ride her horses, play with their dogs and relax on the porch, enjoying the rolling hills of her home south of Nashville. Country music is a passion of hers and she loves to listen to it while she writes, although when she writes sex scenes, it has to be completely quiet.

She is an avid reader of romance novels and enjoys reading Nora Roberts, Jude Deveraux and Susan Wiggs. Finding new authors and delving into something different helps feed the need for literature. A registered nurse by education, she loves to help people and spread the enjoyment of romance to those around her with her novels. She loves cowboys so you'll find many of her novels have sexy men in tight jeans and cowboy boots.

Secret Cravings Publishing
www.secretcravingspublishing.com

Made in the USA
Lexington, KY
01 March 2013